Augustus took t
fingers brush h

D0328074

Claimed by a King

Irresistible royal passion!

Meet the powerful rulers of Byzenmaach, Liesendaach, Arun and Thallasia.

Their royal duty must come before everything.

Nothing and *no one* can distract them.

But how can Casimir, Theodosius, Augustus and Valentine deny the fierce flames of desire when they meet the only women ever to threaten their iron resolve?

Read Casimir of Byzenmaach's story in
Shock Heir for the Crown Prince

Read Theodosius of Liesendaach's story in
Convenient Bride for the King

Read Augustus of Arun's story in
Untouched Queen by Royal Command

and look out for Valentine of Thallasia's story, coming soon!

Don't miss this sinful, sexy quartet by Kelly Hunter!

Kelly Hunter

UNTOUCHED QUEEN BY ROYAL COMMAND

HARLEQUIN PRESENTS®

Recycling programs
for this product may
not exist in your area.

ISBN-13: 978-1-335-53809-3

Untouched Queen by Royal Command

First North American publication 2019

Printed in U.S.A.

Kelly Hunter has always had a weakness for fairy tales, fantasy worlds and losing herself in a good book. She has two children, avoids cooking and cleaning and, despite the best efforts of her family, is no sports fan. Kelly is, however, a keen gardener and has a fondness for roses. Kelly was born in Australia and has traveled extensively. Although she enjoys living and working in different parts of the world, she still calls Australia home.

Books by Kelly Hunter

Harlequin Presents

Claimed by a King

Shock Heir for the Crown Prince
Convenient Bride for the King

Visit the Author Profile page
at Harlequin.com for more titles.

PROLOGUE

Augustus

THEY WEREN'T SUPPOSED to be in this part of the palace. Fourteen-year-old Augustus, Crown Prince of Arun, had been looking for the round room with the domed glass roof for at least six years. He could see that roof from the helicopter every time they flew in or out, but he'd never been able to find the room and no adult had ever been willing to help him out.

His father said that those quarters had been mothballed over a hundred years ago.

His mother said it was out of bounds because the roof was unsafe.

Didn't stop him and his sister looking for it, even if they never had much luck. It was like a treasure hunt.

They wouldn't have found it this time either, without the help of a map.

The floor was made of moon-coloured marble, and so too were the columns and archways surrounding the central room. The remaining furniture had been covered with dusty drapes that had probably once been white. Above all, it felt warm in a way that the main castle living areas were never warm.

'Why do we not live in *this* part of the palace?' asked his sister from somewhere not far behind him. She'd taken to opening every door of every room that circled the main area. 'These look like bedrooms. I could live here.'

'You want fifty bedrooms all to yourself?'

'I want to curl up like a cat in the sunlight. Show me one other place in the palace where you can do that.'

'Mother would kill you if you took to lounging about in the sun. You'd lose your milky-white complexion.'

'Augustus, I don't *have* a milky-white complexion—no matter what our mother might want. I have black hair, black eyes and olive skin—just like you and Father do. My skin likes the sun. It *needs* the sun, it *craves* the sun. Oh, wow.' She'd disappeared through another marble archway and her voice echoed faintly. 'Indoor pool.'

'What?' He backtracked and headed for the

archway, bumping into his sister, who was backing up fast.

'Something rustled in the corner,' she muttered by way of explanation.

'Still want to live here?' He couldn't decide whether the hole in the ground was big enough to be called a pool or small enough to be called a bath. All he knew was that he'd never seen mosaic floor tiles with such elaborate patterns before, and he'd never seen exactly that shade of blue.

'I still want to look around,' his sister offered. 'But you can go first.'

He rolled his eyes, even as pride demanded he take the lead. He'd been born to rule a country one day, after all. A rustling sound would not defeat him. He swaggered past his sister and turned to the right. There was a sink for washing hands carved into the wall beside the archway, and taps that gleamed with a dull silver glow. He reached for one and, with some effort, got it to turn but there was no water. Not a gurgle, a splutter or even the clank of old pipes.

'What is this place? What are all these stone benches and alcoves for?' his sister asked as she followed him into the room. She kept a wary eye on the shadowy corners but eventually turned her attention to other parts of the room.

It was an old map of the palace that had guided them here. That and a history teacher who preferred giving his two royal students books to read so that he could then nap his way through afternoon lessons. Their loss. And sometimes their freedom. If they got caught in here, he could probably even spin it that they were continuing their history lesson hands-on.

'Maybe it was built for a company of warrior knights who slept in the rooms and came here to bathe. They could have practised sword-fighting in the round room,' his sister suggested.

'Maybe.'

Kings had ruled from this palace stronghold for centuries. It was why the place looked so formidable from the outside and had relatively few creature comforts on the inside, no matter how many generations of royals had tried to make it more liveable. There was something about it that resisted softening. Except for in here. There was something soft and strangely beautiful about this part of the palace. Augustus plucked at a scrap of golden silk hanging from a peg on a wall and watched it fall in rotting pieces to the floor. 'Did knights wear embroidered silk bathrobes?'

His sister glanced over and gasped. 'Did you just destroy that?'

'No, I moved it. Time destroyed it.' Rational argument was his friend.

'Can I have some?'

Without waiting for permission, she scooped the rotting cloth from the floor, bunched it in her hand and began to rub at a nearby tile.

'It's going to take a little more than that to get this place clean.'

'I just want to see the pictures,' his sister grumbled, and then, 'Oh.' She stopped cleaning.

He looked, and…oh. 'Congratulations. You found the ancient tile porn.'

'It's *art*, you moron.'

'Uh-huh.'

'I wish we could see better in here,' his sister said.

'For that we would need electricity. Or burning torches for all the holders in the walls.' He closed his eyes and a picture came to mind, clear as day. Not knights and warriors living in this part of the palace and bathing in this room, but women, bound in service to the reigning King.

Augustus had never read about any of his ancestors having a harem, but then, as their eighty-year-old history teacher was fond of telling them, not all facts made it into their history books. 'So, bedrooms, communal bathing room, big gathering room…what else?'

There were more rooms leading from the centre dome. An ancient kitchen, storage rooms with bare shelves, larger rooms with fireplaces, smaller rooms with candle stubs still sitting in carved-out hollows in the walls. They found chests of drawers and sideboards beneath heavy canvas cloth, long mirrors that his sister swore made her look thinner, and even an old hairbrush.

'I don't think people even know this stuff is here,' Moriana said as she put the brush gently back into place. 'I don't know *why* they're ignoring it. Some of it's really old. Museum-old. The back of this brush looks like ivory, inlaid with silver, and it's just been abandoned. Maybe we should bring the history prof down here. He'd have a ball.'

'No.' His voice came out sharper than he meant it to. 'This is a private place. He doesn't get to come here.'

Moriana glanced at him warily but made no comment as they left the side room they'd been exploring.

All doorways and arches led back to the

main room. It was like a mini town square—or town circle. He looked up at the almost magical glass ceiling. 'Maybe our forefathers studied the stars from here. Mapped them.' Perhaps he could come back one night and do the same. And if he took another look at those naked people tiles in the room with the empty pool, so be it. Even future kings had to get their information from somewhere. 'Maybe they hung a big telescope from the ropes up there and moved it around. Maybe if they climbed the stairs over there…' He gestured towards the stairs that ran halfway up the wall and ended in a stone landing with not a railing in sight. 'Maybe they had pulleys and ropes that shifted stuff. Maybe this was a place for astronomers.'

'Augustus, that's a circus trapeze.'

'You think they kept a circus in here?'

'I think this is a harem.'

So much for his innocent little sister not guessing what this place had once been. 'I'm going up the stairs. Coming?'

Moriana followed him. She didn't always agree with him but she could always be counted on to be there for him at the pointy end of things. It didn't help that their mother praised Augustus to the skies for his sharp mind and impeccable self-control, and never failed to criticise Moriana's emotional excesses. As far as Augustus could tell, he was just as fiery as his sister, maybe more so. He was just better at turning hot temper into icy, impenetrable regard.

A king must always put the needs of his people before his own desires.

His father's words. Words to live by. Words to rule by.

A king must never lose control.

Words to *be* ruled by, whether he wanted to be ruled by them or not.

They made it to the ledge and he made his sister sit rather than stand. He sat too, his back to the wall as he looked up to the roof and then down at the intricately patterned marble floor.

'I feel like a bird in a cage,' said Moriana. 'Wonder what the women who once lived here felt like?'

'Sounds about right.' He wasn't a woman but he knew what being trapped by duty felt like.

'We could practise our archery from up here.' Moriana made fists out in front of her and drew back one arm as if pulling back an imaginary arrow. 'Set up targets down below. *Pfft.* Practise our aim.'

'Bloodthirsty. I like it.' Bottled-up anger had to go somewhere. He could use this place at other times too. Get away from the eyes that watched and judged his every move. 'Swear to me you won't tell anyone that we've been here.'

'I swear.' Her eyes gleamed.

'And that you won't come here by yourself.'

'Why not? You're going to.'

Sometimes his sister was a mind-reader.

'What are you going to do here all by yourself?' she wanted to know.

Roar. Weep. Let everything out that he felt compelled to keep in. 'Don't you ever want to be some place where no one's watching and judging your every move? Sit in the sun if you want to sit in the sun. Lose your temper and finally say all those things you want to say, even if no one's listening. Especially because no one's listening.' Strip back the layers of caution and restraint he clothed himself in and see what was underneath. Even if it was all selfish and ugly and wrong. 'I need somewhere to go where I'm free to be myself. This could be that place.'

His sister brought her knees to her chest and wrapped her arms around her legs. The gaze she turned on him was troubled. 'We shouldn't have to hide our real selves from everyone, Augustus. I know we're figureheads but surely we can let *some* people see what's underneath.'

'Yeah, well.' He thought back to the hour-long lecture on selfishness he'd received for daring to tell his father that he didn't want to attend yet another state funeral for a king he'd never met. 'You're not me.'

Sera

Sera wasn't supposed to leave the house when her mother's guest was visiting. Stay in the back room, keep quiet, don't ever be seen. Those were the rules and seven-year-old Sera knew better than to break them. Three times a week, maybe four, the visitor would come to her mother's front door and afterwards there might be food for the table and wine for her mother, although these days there was more wine and less food. Her mother was sick and the wine was like medicine, and her sweet, soft-spoken mother smelled sour now and the visitor never stayed long.

Sera's stomach grumbled as she went to the door between the living room and the rest of the once grand house and put her ear to it. If she got to the bakery before closing time there might be a loaf of bread left and the baker would give it to her for half price, and a sweet bun to go with it. The bread wasn't always fresh but the sweet treat was always free and once there'd even been eggs. The baker always said, 'And wish your mother a good day from me'. Her mother always smiled and said the baker was a Good Man.

Her mother had gone to school with him and they'd played together as children, long before her mother had gone away to learn and train and become something more.

Sera didn't know what her mother meant by *more*; all she knew was that there weren't many things left in their house to sell and her mother was sick all the time now and didn't laugh any more unless there was wine and then she would laugh at nothing at all. Whatever her mother had once been: a dancer, a lady, someone who could make Sera's nightmares go away at the touch of her hand…she wasn't that same person any more.

Every kid in the neighbourhood knew what she was now, including Sera.

Her mother was a whore.

There was no noise coming from the other room. No talking, no laughter, no…other. Surely the visitor would be gone by now? The light was fading outside. The baker would close his shop soon and there would be no chance of bread at all.

She heard a thud, as if someone had bumped into furniture, followed by the tinkle of breaking glass. Her mother had dropped wine glasses before and it was Sera's job to pick up the pieces and try to make her mother sit down instead of dancing around and leaving sticky bloody footprints on the old wooden floor, and all the time telling Sera she was such a good, good girl.

Some of those footprints were still there. Stuck in the wood with no rugs to cover them.

The rugs had all been sold.

No sound at all as Sera inched the door open and put her eye to the crack, and her mother was kneeling and picking up glass, and most importantly she was alone. Sera pushed the door open and was halfway across the room before she saw the other person standing in front of the stone-cold fireplace. She stopped, frozen. Not the man but still a visitor: a woman dressed in fine clothes and it was hard to look away from her. She reminded Sera of what her mother had once been: all smooth and beautiful lines, with clear eyes and a smile that made her feel warm.

Sera looked towards her mother for direction now that the rule had been broken, not daring to speak, not daring to move, even though there was still glass on the floor that her mother had missed.

'We don't need you,' her mother said, standing up and then looking away. 'Go home.'

Home *where*?

'My neighbour's girl,' her mother told the visitor. 'She cleans here.'

'Then you'd best let her do it.'

'I can do it.' Her mother stared coldly at the other woman before turning back to Sera. 'Go. Come back tomorrow.'

'Wait,' said the visitor, and Sera stood, torn, while the visitor came closer and put a gentle hand to Sera's face and turned it towards the light. 'She's yours.'

'No, I—'

'Don't lie. She's yours.'

Her mother said nothing.

'You broke the rules,' the older woman said.

Sera whispered, 'I'm sorry…'

At the same time her mother said, 'I fell in *love*.'

And then her mother laughed harshly and it turned into a sob, and the older woman straightened and turned towards the sound.

'You didn't have to leave,' the older woman said gently. 'There are ways—'

'No.'

'You're one of us. We would have taken care of you.'

Her mother shook her head. No and no. 'Ended us both.'

'*Hidden* you both,' said the older woman. 'Do you really think you're the first courtesan to ever fall in love and beget a child?'

Sera bent to the task of picking up glass shards from the floor, trying to make herself as small as she could, trying to make them forget she was there so she could hear them talk more, never mind that she didn't understand what half the words meant.

'How did you find us?' her mother asked.

'Serendipity.' Another word Sera didn't know. 'I was passing through the town and stopped at the bakery for a sourdough loaf,' the older woman said with a faint smile. 'Mainly because in all the world there's none as good as the ones they make there. The baker's boy remembered me. He's the baker now, as I expect you know, and he mentioned you. We talked. I mean you no harm. I want to help.'

'You can't. I'm beyond help now.'

'Then let me help your daughter.'

'How? By training her to serve and love others and never ask for anything in return? I will *never* choose that life for my daughter.'

'You liked it well enough once.'

'I was a fool.'

'And are you still a fool? What do you think will happen to the child once you poison your body with drink and starve yourself to death? Who will care for her, put a roof over her head and food in her mouth, educate her and give her a sense of self-worth?'

Mama looked close to crying. 'Not you.'

'I don't see many choices left to you.' The woman glanced around the room. 'Unless I'm mistaken, you've already sold everything of value. Any jewellery left?'

'No.' Sera could hardly hear her mother's answer.

'Does the house belong to you?'

'No.'

'How long have you been ill?'

'A year. Maybe more. I'm not—it's not—catching. It's cancer.'

The older woman bowed her head. 'And how much longer do you think you can last, selling your favours to the lowest bidder? How long before he looks towards the girl and wants her instead of you? Yuna, please. I can give you a home again. *Treatment* if there's treatment to be had. Comfort and clothing befitting your status and hers. Complete discretion when it comes to *whose* child she is—don't think I don't know.'

'He won't want her.'

'You're right, he won't. But I do. The Order of the Kite will always look after its own. From the fiercest hawk to the fallen sparrow. How can you not know this?'

A tear slipped beneath her mother's closed lashes. 'I thought I'd be better off away from it all. For a while it was good. It can be good again.'

'Do you really believe that?' The older woman crossed to her mother and took hold of her hands. 'Let me help you.'

'Promise me she won't be trained as a courtesan,' her mother begged. 'Lianthe, *please*.'

'I promise to give her the same choice I gave you.'

'You'll dazzle her.'

'You'll counter that.' The older woman drew Sera's mother towards the couch, not letting go of her hands, even after they were both seated. Sera edged closer, scared of letting the hem of the woman's gown get in the puddle of wine on the floor, and loving the sweet, clean smell that surrounded her. The woman smiled. 'Leave it, child. Come, let me look at you.'

Sera withstood the other woman's gaze for

as long as she could. *Stand tall, chin up, don't fidget.* Her mother's words ringing in her mind. *No need to look like a street urchin.*

Fidget, fidget, beneath the woman's quiet gaze.

'My name's Lianthe,' the woman said finally. 'And I want you and your mother to come to my home in the mountains so that I can take care of you both until your mother is well again. Would you like that?'

'Would there be visitors for Mama?'

'What kind of visitors?'

'The man.'

Her mother and the lady shared a long glance.

'He would not visit. I would be taking you too far away for that.'

'Would there be wine for her?' Because wine was important. 'Wine's like medicine.'

'Then there will be wine until we find better medicine. Tell me, child, are you hungry?'

So, so hungry but she'd learned long ago that sometimes it was better to say nothing than to give the wrong answer. Her stomach grumbled the answer for her anyway.

'When did you last eat?' the lady asked next.

Same question. Trick question. 'Would you like some tea?' Sera asked anxiously. There was tea in the cupboard and Mama always offered visitors a drink. Tea was a warm drink. She knew how to make it and what cups to use. There was a tray. 'I could bring you some tea.'

The lady looked towards her mother as if she'd done something wrong. Something far worse than forgetting to lock the door or not turn off the bedroom lamp at night. 'Yuna, what are you doing? You're already training her in the ways of self-sacrifice and denial. It's too soon for that. You know it is.'

Another tear slipped silently down her mother's face. Lianthe's gaze hardened.

'And now she looks to you for guidance and approval. Yuna, you *must* see what you're doing here. This isn't freedom. This isn't childhood as it's meant to be lived. This is abuse and, of all the things we taught you, no member of the Order ever taught you that.'

'He's not to know,' her mother said raggedly. 'He's not to take her.'

'He will never know. This I promise.'

'She's not to be sent anywhere near him.'

'You have my word.'

'She gets to choose. If she doesn't want to be a companion, you set her up to succeed elsewhere.'

'Agreed.'

'Sera?' Her mother asked her name as a question but Sera stayed quiet and paid attention because she didn't yet know what the question was. 'Should we go to the mountains with the Lady Lianthe? Would you like that?'

Away from here and the baker who was a Good Man and the kids who called her names and the men who looked at her with eyes that burned hot and hungry. Away from the fear that her mother would one day go to sleep on a belly full of wine and never wake up. 'Would there be food? And someone to take care of us?'

Her mother buried her face in her hands.

'Yes, there will be food and people who will care for you both,' the Lady Lianthe said. 'Sera. Is that your name?'

Sera nodded.

'Pretty name.' The woman's smile wrapped around her like a blanket. 'Pretty girl.'

CHAPTER ONE

SHE WAS A gift from her people to the King of Arun. An unwanted gift if the King's expression spoke true, but one he couldn't refuse. Not without breaking the laws of his country and severing seven centuries of tradition between his people and hers. Sera observed him through a veil of lashes and the protection afforded by her hooded travelling cloak. He could not refuse her.

Although he seemed to be considering it.

She was a courtesan, born, bred and shaped for the King's entertainment. Pledged into service at the age of seven in return for the finest food, shelter and an education second to none. Chosen for the beauty she possessed and the quickness of her mind. Taught to serve, to soothe, and how to dance, fight and dress. One for every King of Arun and only one. A possession to be treasured.

She stood before him, ready to serve. She wasn't unwilling. She'd already received far more from the bargain than she'd ever given and if it was time to pay up, so be it.

He was a handsome man if a tall, lean frame, firm lips, a stern jaw and wayward dark hair appealed—which it did. He had a reputation for fair and thoughtful leadership.

She definitely wasn't unwilling.

He looked relaxed as his gaze swept over her party. Two warriors stood to attention either side of her and another watched her back. The Lady Lianthe, elder spokeswoman for the High Reaches, preceded her. A party of five—with her in the centre, protected—they faced the Arunian King, who stood beside a tall leather chair in a room too cold and bleak for general living.

The old courtier who had guided them to the reception room finally spoke. 'Your Majesty, the Lady Lianthe, elder stateswoman of the High Reaches. And party.'

He knew who they were for they'd applied for this audience days ago. His office had been sent a copy of the accord. Sera wondered whether he'd spent the past two days poring over old diaries and history books in an effort to understand what none of his forefathers had seen fit to teach him.

He had a softness for women, this King, for all that he had taken no wife. He'd held his mother in high regard when she was alive, although she'd been dead now for many years. He held his recently married sister, Queen Consort of Liesendaach, in high esteem still. His name had been linked to several eligible women, although nothing had ever come of it.

'So it's time,' he said, and Sera almost smiled. She'd studied his speeches and knew that voice well. The cultured baritone weight of it and the occasional icy edge that could burn deeper than flame. There was no ice in it yet.

Lianthe rose from her curtsey and inclined her head. 'Your Majesty, as per the accord afforded our people by the Crown in the year thirteen twelve—'

'I don't want her.'

Lianthe's composure never wavered. They'd practised for this moment and every variation of it. At the King's interruption, the elder stateswoman merely started again. 'As per the accord, and in the event the King of Arun remains unmarried into his majority, the people of the High Reaches shall provide unto him a concubine of noble birth—'

'I cannot accept.'

'A concubine of noble birth, charged with attending the King's needs and demands until such time as he acquires a wife and produces an heir. Thereafter, and at the King's discretion—'

'She cannot stay here.' Finally, the ice had entered his voice. Not that it would do him any good. The people of the High Reaches had a duty to fulfil.

'Thereafter, and at the King's discretion, she shall be released from service, gifted her weight in gold and returned to her people.'

There it was, the accord read in full, a concubine presented and a duty discharged. Sera watched, from within the shadows her travelling hood afforded her, as Lianthe clasped her bony hands in front of her and tried to look less irritated and more accommodating.

'The accord stands, Your Majesty,' Lianthe reminded him quietly. 'It has never been dissolved.'

The King's black gaze swept from the older woman to rest broodingly on Sera's cloaked form. She could feel the weight of his regard and the displeasure in it. 'Lady Lianthe, with all due respect to the people of the High Reaches, I have no intention of being bound by this arrangement. Concubines have no place here. Not in this day and age.'

'With all due respect, you know nothing of concubines.' Fact and reprimand all rolled into one. 'By all means petition the court, your parliament and the church. Many have tried. All have failed. We can wait. Meanwhile, we all do what we must. Your Majesty, it is my duty and honour to present to you the Lady Sera Boreas, daughter of Yuna, Courtesan of the High Reaches and valued member of the Order of the Kite. Our gift to you.' Lianthe paused delicately. 'In your time of need.'

Sera hid her smile and sank to the floor in a curtsey, her head lowered and her cloak pooling around her like a black stain. Lianthe was not amused by their welcome, that much was clear to anyone with ears. This new King knew nothing of the role Sera might occupy if given the chance. What she could do for him. How best he might harness her skills. He didn't want her.

More fool him.

He didn't bid her to rise so she stayed down until he did. Cold, this grey stone hall with its too-righteous King. Pettiness did not become him.

'Up,' he said finally and Sera risked a glance

at Lianthe as she rose. The older woman's eyes flashed silver and her lips thinned.

'Your Majesty, you appear to be mistaking the Lady Sera for a pet.'

'Probably because you insist on giving her away as if she is one,' he countered drily. 'I've read the housing requirements traditionally afforded the concubines of the north. I do hope you can supply your own eunuchs. I'm afraid I don't have any to hand.' His gaze swept over the warriors of the High Reaches and they stared back, eyes hard and unmoving. 'No eunuchs accompany you at the moment, I'd wager,' he said quietly.

He wasn't wrong. 'I can make do without if you can, Your Majesty.' Sera let warm amusement coat her voice. 'However, I do look forward to occupying the living quarters traditionally offered the concubines from the north. I've read a lot about the space.'

'Is there a face to match that honeyed voice?' he asked, after a pause that spanned a measured breath or four.

She raised her hands and pushed her travelling hood from her face. His eyes narrowed. Reluctant amusement teased at his lips. 'You might want to lead with that face, next time,' he said.

Sera had not been chosen for her plainness of form. 'As long as it pleases you, Your Majesty.'

'I'm sure it pleases everyone.' There might just be a sense of humour in there somewhere. 'Lady Sera, how exactly do you expect to be of use to me?'

'It depends what you need.'

'I need you gone.'

'Ah.' The man was decidedly single-minded. Sera inclined her head in tacit agreement. 'In that case you need a wife, Your Majesty. Would you like me to find you one?'

Augustus, King of Arun, was no stranger to the machinations of women, but he'd never—in all his years—encountered women like these. One cloaked in a rich, regal red, her beauty still a force to be reckoned with, never mind her elder status. The other cloaked in deepest black from the neck down, her every feature perfect and her eyes a clear and bitter grey. Neither woman seemed at all perturbed by his displeasure or by the words spilling from their lips.

He was used to having people around who did his bidding, but he called them employees, not servants, and there were rules and guidelines governing what he expected of them and what they could expect from him.

There were no clear rules for this.

He and his aides had spent the last two days in the palace record rooms, scouring the stacks for anything that mentioned the concubines of the High Reaches and the laws governing them. So far, he'd found plenty of information about their grace, beauty and unrivalled manners. So far, he'd found nothing to help him get rid of them.

A concubine of the High Reaches was a gift to be unwrapped with the care one might afford a poisoned chalice, one of his ancestor Kings had written. Not exactly reassuring.

'These living quarters you've read about…' He shook his head and allowed a frown. 'They've been mothballed for over a hundred and twenty years.' As children, he and his sister had been fascinated by the huge round room with the ribbed glass ceiling. Right up until his mother had caught them in there one day, staging a mock aerial war on a dozen vicious pumpkins. She'd had that place locked down so fast and put a guard detail on the passageway into it and that had been the end of his secret retreat. 'There's no modern heating, no electricity, and the water that used to run into the pools there has long since been diverted. The space is not fit for use.'

'The people of the High Reaches are not without resources,' said the elder stateswoman regally. 'It would be our honour to restore the living area to its former glory.'

They had an answer for everything. 'Don't get too comfortable,' he warned and looked towards his executive secretary. 'Let all bear witness that the terms of the accord have been satisfied. Let it also be recorded that my intention is to see the Lady Sera honourably discharged from her duty as quickly as possible. I'll find my own wife in my own good time and have no need of a concubine.' He was only thirty. Wasn't as if he was *that* remiss when it came to begetting an heir and securing the throne. His sister could rule if it ever came to that. Her children could rule, although her husband, Theo, would doubtless object. Neighbouring Liesendaach needed an heir too, perhaps even more so than Arun did. He nodded towards his secretary. 'Show them the hospitality they've requested.'

If the abandoned round room didn't make them flinch, nothing would.

The guards bowed and the women curtseyed, all of it effortlessly choreographed as they turned and swept from the room, leaving only silence behind. Silence and the lingering scent of violets.

Sera waited just outside the door for Lianthe to fall into step with her. Two guards and their guide up ahead and another guard behind them, a familiar routine in an unfamiliar place.

'That could have gone better,' Sera murmured.

'Insolent whelp,' said the older woman with enough bite to make the stone walls crumble.

'Me?'

'Him. No wonder he isn't wed.'

The King's secretary coughed, up ahead.

'Yes, it's extremely damp down here,' offered Lianthe. 'Although I dare say the rats enjoy it.'

'We're taking a short cut, milady. Largely unused,' the man offered. 'As for the rooms issued for the Lady Sera's use, I know not what to say. You'll find no comfort there. The palace has many other suites available for guests. You have but to ask for different quarters and they'll be provided.'

He opened a door and there was sunshine and a small walled courtyard stuffed with large pots of neatly kept kitchen herbs. Who-

ever tended this garden knew what they were
about. Another door on the other side of the
little courtyard plunged them into dankness
once more before the corridor widened enough
to allow for half a dozen people to walk comfortably side by side. At the end of the corridor
stood a pair of huge doors wrought in black
wood with iron hinges. Two thick wooden
beams barred the door closed.

The old guide stood aside and looked to the
High Reaches guards. 'Well? What are you
waiting for?'

'*Very* welcoming,' murmured Sera as the
guards pushed against the bindings and ancient wood and metal groaned. 'Perhaps some
plinths and flowers either side might brighten
this entrance hall? Discreet lighting. Scented
roses.'

With another strangled cough from their
guide, the bars slid to the side and the doors
were pushed open. A soaring glass-domed
space the size of a cathedral apse greeted
them, encircled by grey marble columns and
shadowy alcoves. What furniture remained
lay shrouded beneath dust sheets and if rugs
had once graced the vast expanse of grey stone
floor they certainly weren't in evidence now.
Dust motes danced in the air at the disturbance

from the opening of the doors, and was that a dovecote in one of the alcoves or a postbox for fifty? Another alcove contained the bathing pool, empty but for dirt, but the plumbing had worked once and would work again—it was her job to see to it. There were faded frescoes on the walls and a second floor with a cloistered walkway that looked down on the central area. Chandeliers still hung in place, struggling to shine beneath decades of dust. There was even a circus trapeze roped carelessly to a tiny balcony set one floor above the rest. Illustrations in the journals of the courtesans of old had not done the place justice.

'Well, now.' Sera sent a fleeting smile in Lianthe's direction. 'Nothing like a challenge.'

The older woman nodded and turned to their guide. 'Can you offer us cleaners?' The man looked unsure. 'No? Then we shall invite our own, and tradespeople too. I suppose we should thank the monarchy for preserving the space in all its historical glory. At least there are no rats.'

'And I think I know why.' Sera stared up at the domed glass ceiling to where several lumpy shapes sat, nestled into the framework. 'Are they owls?'

Lianthe looked up and smiled. 'Why, yes. A

good omen, don't you think? Would you like to keep them?'

'Depends on the rats.' Call her difficult but if the rats were gone Sera was all for providing alternative living space—and hunting options—for the raptors. 'We may need the assistance of a falconer. I don't suppose King Augustus keeps one of those any more either?'

'No, Lady Sera. But King Casimir of Byzenmaach does,' said their guide.

'Ah, yes.' Lianthe nodded. 'The falconers of Byzenmaach are men of legend and steeped in the old ways. Tomas-the-Tongue-Tied is head falconer there these days is he not? How is the boy?'

'Grown, milady, although still somewhat tongue-tied,' said the old guide and won a rare smile from Lianthe. 'But ever devoted to his winged beasts. If you need him here, we can get him here.'

'Wonderful,' said Sera. Eyes on the prize, or, in this case, the speedy removal of hunting birds from her future living quarters. 'Let's aim for that. Unless by "Don't get too comfortable" King Augustus meant for me to sleep with the wildlife? Perhaps I should go back and ask.'

'You must definitely ask,' said Lianthe.

It was decided. Sera shed her travelling cloak and watched the old courtier blink and then raise his hand as if to shade his eyes from the glare. Granted her dainty six-inch heels were a burnt orange colour and her slimline ankle-length trousers were only one shade darker, but her tunic was a meek ivory chiffon and the gold metal bustier beneath it covered far more than usual and ran all the way up and around her neck.

'Something wrong?' she asked the old guide.

'Headache,' he said, and touched two fingers to his temple.

'I know massage techniques for that,' she began. 'Very effective. Would you like me to—'

'*No*, milady. No! You just...' He waved his arm in the air ineffectually. 'Go and see Augustus. The King. King Augustus.'

'I know who you mean,' she said gently, sharing a concerned glance with Lianthe. 'Are you quite well? I'd offer you a seat if I could find one. Or a drink. Would you like me to call for water?'

'No, milady. I'm quite recovered.'

But he still looked painfully pinched and long-suffering. 'Is it the jewels? Because the bustier isn't quite my normal attire. It's part of the courtesan's chest.'

'It certainly seems that way, milady. I must confess, I wasn't expecting the bejewelled wrist and ankle cuffs either.'

Ah. 'Well, they are very beautiful. And surprisingly light given all the bronze and amber inlays and gold filigree. There are chains to go with them,' she said.

'Of course there are.' The man's fingers went to massage his temple again.

'Will I find the King in the same place we left him?' asked Sera, because sometimes it paid to be practical.

'He may be back in his office by now. Two doors to the left of the room you met him in. The outer area houses the secretary's desk. The secretary's not there because that would be me and I am here. The inner room is his, and the door to it may or may not be open. Either way, knock.'

Sera found the King exactly where the old courtier said he would be; the door through to his office was open and she paused to check her posture before knocking gently on the door frame. He lifted his gaze from the papers on the big black table in front of him and blinked. And blinked again.

She curtseyed again, all but kissing the floor, because this man was her King and protocol demanded it.

'Up,' he said, with a slight tinge of weariness. 'What is it?'

Not *Come in*, so she stayed in the doorway. 'I want to invite Tomas the Byzenmaach falconer to call on me.'

'Tired of me already?' He arched an eyebrow, even as he studied her intently, starting with her shoes and seeming to get stuck in the general vicinity of her chest. The golden bustier was quite arresting but not the most comfortable item of clothing she owned. 'That was quick.'

'I need him here so he can remove the raptors from my quarters.'

'Raptors as in dinosaurs? Because it's been that kind of day.'

'Raptors as in owls.'

'I'm almost disappointed,' he said, and there was humour in him, sharp and slippery. 'What is that you're wearing, exactly? Apart from the clothes. Which I appreciate, by the way. Clothes are useful. You'll get cold here if you don't wear more of them.'

'You mean the jewellery? Your secretary seemed very taken by it as well. It's ceremonial, for the most part, although practical too.'

'Practical?'

'D-rings and everything.' She held up one wrist and showed him the loop and then pointed to another where the bustier came to-gether at the back of her neck. 'So do I have your permission to call in the falconer?'

'Is this a plea for different living quarters? Because I'm being as clear as I can be here. I don't want to give you *any* quarters, but, given that I *must*, you are welcome to more suitable living arrangements than the ones you have requested. I would not deny you that.'

'It's not a plea for new quarters.' He tested her patience, this King with the giant stick up his rear. 'And, yes, you're being very clear. Per-haps I should be equally clear.' Save herself a few meetings with him in the process. 'I want your permission to clean and ready my living quarters for use. I will call in experts, when necessary. I will see the courtesan's lodgings restored and it will cost you and the palace nothing. I will take all care to preserve the history of the rooms—more care than you or your people would. I will submit names, on a daily basis, of each and every craftsperson or cleaning person that I bring in. By your leave, and provided I have free rein to do so, I can have those rooms fit to live in within a week. Do I have your permission?'

'You argue like a politician. All fine words, sketchy rationale and promises you'll never keep.'

'I'll keep this promise, Your Majesty. Consider this a test if you need a reason to say yes.'

'And when you leave again? What happens to all these home improvements then?'

'I expect the next courtesan will benefit from them.'

'Sera.' He spoke quietly but with an authority that ran bone-deep, and it got to her in a way the authority of her teachers never had. 'There's not going to be another courtesan delivered to a King of Arun. This I promise.'

'Then turn the place into a museum,' she snapped, defiant in the face of extinction. 'You don't value me. I get it. You don't need my help, you don't want my help, and you don't understand the *backing* you've just been blessed with. So be it. Meanwhile, we're both bound by tradition and moreover I have dues to pay. Do I have your permission to engage the help I need to make my living quarters habitable?'

'And here I thought courtesans were meant to be compliant.'

'I am compliant.' She could be so meekly

compliant his head would spin. 'I can be whatever you want me to be. All I need is direction.'

His face did not betray his thoughts. Not by the flicker of an eye or the twitching of a muscle.

'You have my permission to make your living quarters habitable,' he said finally. 'And Sera?'

She waited.

'Don't ever walk the halls of my palace in your ancient slave uniform again.'

The King's secretary had gone by the time Sera arrived back in the quarters she'd claimed as her own. She held her head high as she entered, never mind that the chill in the air and the ice in the King's eyes had turned her skin to gooseflesh. She wouldn't cry, she never had—not even at her mother's funeral—but the gigantic task of readying this space for use and earning Augustus of Arun's trust, and, yes, finding him a wife, was daunting enough to make her smile falter and her shoulders droop as she stared around at her new home.

Lianthe and the guards had already begun pulling covers off the furnishings and for that she would be grateful. She wasn't alone in this. Other people had faith in her abilities.

'I've already sent for cleaning equipment and linens,' Lianthe said when she saw her. 'Did you find him again?'

'I did.'

'And?'

'He's a funny guy. He's also hard as nails underneath, doesn't like not getting his own way and he's going to be hell on my sense of self-worth.'

'We knew this wasn't going to be an easy sell. I'm sure you'll come to a greater understanding of each other eventually.'

'I'm glad someone's sure,' she murmured.

'And what did he have to say about securing a falconer to help get rid of our feathered friends?'

'Oh, that?' She'd forgotten about that. 'He said yes.'

CHAPTER TWO

SIX DAYS LATER, Augustus was no closer to a solution when it came to removing his unwanted gift from the palace. He'd kept his distance, stuck to his routine and tried to stay immune to the whispers of the staff as word got around that the palace's pleasure rooms were being refurbished. Ladies Sera and Lianthe had engaged cleaning staff and craftspeople to help with the repairs. Stonemasons had been brought in. Electricity had been restored. Structural engineers had been and gone, proclaiming the glass-domed roof still fit for purpose, with only minor repair required.

Tomas the falconer had come for the owls and brought King Casimir of Byzenmaach's sister Claudia with him. Apparently Sera and Claudia had gone to school together. Sera had prepared a lavish dinner for them that had gone on for hours. They'd caught up on each other's lives. Swapped stories. Augustus had been invited.

He hadn't attended.

Whispers turned into rumours, each one more fanciful than the rest.

The Lady Sera was a sorceress, a witch, an enchantress and his apparent downfall. Her eyes were, variously, the softest dove-grey and as kind as an angel's or as bleak as the winter sky and hard as stone. She and her guards danced with swords beneath the dome, and splattered reflected sunlight across the walls with uncanny precision, so the cleaners said. She'd had the trapeze taken down only to replace it with another, and this time the trapeze fluttered with silks that fell to the floor, his secretary told him.

Silks she climbed up and down as if they were steps.

Yesterday, a convoy of heavily guarded trucks had arrived from the north and requested entry, sending palace security into a spin and Augustus into a rare temper. *Don't get too comfortable*, he'd said. He would find a way to undo this, he'd said. They *knew* he was working on it. They had no need for deliveries full of priceless artworks only ever revealed when a courtesan of the High Reaches was in residence at the palace.

Even the palace *walls* were buzzing.

Augustus's father, former King and still an advisor to the throne, had been no help. He'd been married with two young children by the time he'd reached thirty and no courtesan of the High Reaches had ever come to him. There was no *precedent* for getting rid of one that didn't directly relate to the rules of the accord. A courtesan, once bestowed, could be removed once a wife and heir had been secured and not before. She could be sent elsewhere at the King's bidding but would still retain full ownership...no, not ownership, access...full access to her quarters in the palace.

She had the right to refuse entrance to all but him. She had the right to entertain there but the guest list had to be approved by him. He'd asked for more details when it came to Sera Boreas's background and education and an information file had landed on his desk this morning. She'd studied philosophy, politics and economics at Oxford. She'd taken music lessons in St Petersburg. Dance lessons with members of the National Ballet company of China. Learned martial arts from the monks of the High Reaches. Her origins were shrouded in mystery. Her mother had kept the company of high ranking politicians and dignitaries the world over. Her mother had been a companion, a facilitator, often providing neutral ground where those from opposing political persuasions could meet. Lianthe of the High Reaches might just be her grandmother but that had yet to be verified. The more he read, the less real she became to him.

For all her contacts and endless qualifications, he still didn't know what she *did* except in the vaguest terms.

In the last year alone, and as the youngest representative of the Order of the Kite, she'd graced the dining tables of dozens of world leaders and people of influence. Her reach was truly astonishing.

And he was currently keeping her in the equivalent of his basement.

He needed to talk with her at the very least.

And damn but he needed another woman's opinion.

And then his intercom flashed.

'Your sister's on the phone,' his well-worn secretary said.

'Put her through,' he murmured. Problem solved.

'Augustus, I know you're pining for me, but did you seriously buy a cat?'

'I—what?' Not exactly where his head had been at. Augustus scowled, and not just because his sister's recent marriage had left his palace without a social organiser and him with no clue as to how to find a replacement equally dedicated to the role. 'Who told you that? Theo?'

'He told me I needed to phone you because he'd heard rumours you were all lonely and had acquired a pet. He also mentioned something about a cat. Is it fluffy? Does it pounce? Has it conquered cucumbers yet?'

Theo, King of Liesendaach and neighbouring monarch, was Moriana's new husband. Theo, King of sly manoeuvres, knew exactly what kind of cat Augustus had bought. 'Moriana, let's get something clear. I am not a lonely cat king. I bought a catamaran. An oceangoing, racing catamaran.'

'Ah,' she said. 'Figures. In that case, I have no idea why Theo was so insistent I phone you this morning. We've just returned from visiting Cas and Ana in the Byzenmaach mountains and, by the way, I will *never* tire of the views from that stronghold. More to the point, I got on well with Cas's new bride and his newfound daughter. There's hope for me yet. They did ask me why they hadn't received an invite to your Winter Solstice ball. Strangely, I haven't received my invitation yet either. I left very comprehensive instructions.'

Moriana was the Queen of Checklists. He had no doubt there would be a binder full of colour-coded instructions sitting on a table somewhere. 'Why isn't Marguerite on top of this?' his sister scolded.

'She didn't work out.'

Silence from his sister, the kind of silence that meant she was valiantly trying to keep her opinions to herself. He gave it three, two, one…

'Augustus, you can't keep firing social secretaries after they've been in the role for two weeks!'

'I can if they're selling palace information to the press,' he said grimly.

'Oh.'

'Yes. Oh. There's a new assistant starting Monday. Meanwhile, what do you know about the Order of the Kite?'

'You mean the courtesans?'

'So you do know something about them.'

'I know they existed centuries ago. They were kept in our round room. Like pets.' Moriana paused, and Augustus waited for her to put Theo's comment about him having a pet together with his question and come up with a clue, but she didn't. 'There are some costumes in the collection here that were reputedly worn by them.' Moriana was warming to her theme. 'Gorgeous things. I wouldn't call them gowns exactly—more like adventurous bedwear. The leather one came with a collection of whips.'

'Whips.' No guesses needed as to how some of those courtesans of old acquired their exalted levels of influence. Augustus put two fingers to his temple and closed his eyes, a habit he'd picked up from his secretary, or maybe the old man had picked it up from him. 'So what else do you know about them? Anything from this day and age?'

'These days they're the stuff of legend. There's a children's book in the nursery about them, assuming it's still there. Seven-year-old girl, clever and pretty, gets ripped from the arms of her unloving family and taken to a palace in the sky to learn how to dance and fight and be a spy. Then she meets a King from the Lower Reaches and spies for him and he falls in love with her and they live happily ever after. Ignore the bit where she poisons his barren wife. You should never believe everything you read.'

'Does this book have a name?'

'*The King's Assassin.* It was one of my favourites. Why?'

No one had ever read it to *him*. 'I currently have the Lady Sera Boreas, daughter of Yuna, Order of the Kite, staying in the round room. She arrived last week, as a *gift* from the people of the High Reaches.'

Silence from Moriana the Red, whose temper, once roused, was also the stuff of legend, and then, 'Say that again?'

'There is a courtesan here in the palace and at my service. Yesterday, six truckloads of priceless antiquities turned up. They belong to the Order of the Kite and can only be seen when a courtesan is in residence here. *Now* do I have your attention?'

'Did you say *priceless antiquities*?'

'*Focus*, Moriana. There is a pet concubine in the round room. No—did you just squeal? Don't squeal. Invite her to stay with you. Keep her. Show her the whips. No! Don't show her the whips. I take that back. But find out what she's doing here. Can you do that?'

'Does she have books?' his sister asked. 'I

bet she has history books with her as well. Do you know what this means?'

It probably meant Moriana was about to try and organise an exhibition of antiquities native to courtesans. 'It means I have a problem that I don't know how to solve yet. What exactly am I supposed to do with this woman?'

'Is she beautiful? They were reputedly all rare beauties.'

'That bit's true.'

'Is she smart?'

'I would say so, yes. Also cunning and completely unfathomable.' Keeping her distance and rousing his curiosity, making her presence felt all the more keenly by the simple act of staying out of his way. 'I need you to come here and see what she wants. Befriend her. Gain her confidence. Tell me what she wants.'

'I can be there in a week.'

'I meant today,' he countered.

'Can't. I have a luncheon at twelve, a charity meeting at two, hospital tour at three and then I'm having a private dinner with my beloved husband who I've barely seen all week.'

'Absence makes the heart grow fonder. I'll send the helicopter for you.'

'Or you could talk to her yourself and find out exactly what this woman can do for you.

Can she act as a social secretary, for example? Can she organise the Winter Solstice ball? Courtesans of old were muses, strategists, women of great influence. Think Madame de Pompadour or Theodora from the Byzantine empire. She might be one of those. Give her something to do. Apart from you, obviously.'

'She is not doing me,' he ground out.

'Has she offered?'

She'd arrived wearing a collar and manacles, amongst other things. She'd called herself a courtesan and then she'd ignored him. 'Who the hell knows?'

'Do you—okay, you know what? Never mind, because there are some things sisters simply shouldn't know. Give her the Winter Solstice ball to oversee. I'm serious. Put her to work. See if she truly wants to be of use to you.'

'I'd rather she left.'

'But why? You need a social secretary who wants to do a good job and isn't inclined to sell us out. Talk to her. See what she wants from her role and from you. Your goals might align.'

'What if she doesn't want to be here at all?'

'Then you'll work together to find a way out of this. But not before I've seen all the art and persuaded her to let us photograph and document it, where possible. I can't wait to see it.'

Augustus sighed. Theo really was a bad influence on his sister, who'd once dutifully dedicated herself to serving the Arunian monarchy. These days she shone a light on the already glittering Liesendaach crown and Augustus sorely missed her attention. He did need someone to replace his sister. Someone with a personal stake in taking on the role and making it their own. A wife…he'd been thinking of it. Not doing anything about it, mind, but thinking that soon he would start looking in earnest. Meanwhile, he had a…courtesan…at his disposal. Whatever that meant. Maybe they could renegotiate her job description.

'All right.' There was nothing else for it. 'I'll talk to her.'

It took until mid-afternoon before Augustus made his way to the round room in search of the elusive Sera of the High Reaches. Ignoring her presence and hoping she'd miraculously go away wasn't working for him. Answers on how best to get rid of her were not forthcoming. Moriana thought she might be of use to him and he trusted his sister's judgement in most things. Sera's CV would make any power broker salivate. To have those kind of contacts at his disposal...

And yet he wasn't the type to share power and he didn't trust her motivations one little bit.

So here he was, foul of temper and distinctly lacking in patience as he stood at the closed doors to the round room and eyed the profusion of damask roses and soft greenery with distaste, even as the scent of them conjured memories of cloistered gardens and all things feminine. His mother had enjoyed overseeing the floral arrangements throughout the palace, but she'd not have allowed this flat-out challenge to grim austerity. This tease to stop and sniff and feast the eyes on such unrepentantly fleeting beauty.

With one last scathing glare, Augustus stood firm against the temptation to lean forward and let the scent of the roses envelop him. Instead, he pulled the dangling cord that would announce his arrival at the doors. He heard the faint chime of bells and then nothing. Ten seconds later, he reached for the cord again, and then the door opened and the roses were forgotten.

Never mind the creamy skin and the perfection of her lips, the delicate curve of her cheekbones, the raven-black hair that fell in a thick plait to her waist or those eyes that glistened dove-grey. Today his courtesan wore low-slung loose trousers and a cropped fitted top that clung to her curves like a greedy lover's hand. She was lean and lithe in all the right places, and generously voluptuous in others.

It was a body designed to bring a man to his knees and keep him there for eternity.

She stepped back and dropped her gaze demurely, even as she opened the door wider and sank to the floor in a curtsey, and he might have felt a heel for causing such an action except that she moved like a dancer, fluid and graceful, and he wanted to watch her do it all over again.

'Don't do that.' It was a curt reminder, mostly to himself, that she shouldn't be on her knees in front of him. It gave him too many ideas, all of them sexual.

'My mistake.' She rose as gracefully as she'd gone down in the first place. 'Welcome, Your Majesty. Please forgive my appearance. I wasn't expecting company.'

'What were you doing?' Her skin glowed with a faint sheen of exertion.

'Forms,' she said. 'Martial arts patterns.'

'Don't stop on my account.'

'I can do them any time,' she murmured. 'I'd rather have company.'

He looked around, taking in the now spotless round room, its stone walls and floors covered in tapestries and carpets, oil paintings and silver-edged mirrors. A huge round sofa had been placed in the centre of the room, beneath the domed glass ceiling. The seats faced inwards and there were openings at all four points of the compass. 'Where is everyone?'

'The tradespeople and artisans have gone and the Lady Lianthe with them. My guards are currently in a meeting with your guards about how best to utilise their services, given that standing outside a door that no one ever knocks on is a waste of their time and expertise. The maids have been and gone. There is only me.'

Holding her own in a round room built for hundreds to gather in and bedrooms enough for fifty. 'It's you I've come to see.'

She turned her back on him and led him towards the sofa at the centre of the room. It was leather and studded and looked comfortably soft with age. Pillows and throws had been placed on it at intervals, and the circular floor tapestry framed by the sofa had a stained-glass quality about it, with different scenes to look at depending on where a person sat. 'What is that?'

'On the floor?'

He nodded.

'It's a communication device. Each scene depicts an action: a need or desire, if you will. In older times a visitor to this place—or even another courtesan—would approach this area and in choosing where to sit would telegraph their needs. Those needs would be seen to.'

'Just like that?'

'So they say.'

'And is that the way it's going to work for me?'

'Why don't you sit somewhere and see?'

'Maybe I will.' Maybe he wouldn't. Better all round if he didn't engage, no matter how fascinating the history she brought with her. 'I've been trying to get rid of you.'

'I know that, Your Majesty.' She glanced towards the tapestry. 'Take your time looking at it. Even if you don't plan to use it as directed it's an amazing piece of artistry. I'll make tea.'

He watched as she walked away from him, tracking every curve as if it would somehow allow him to see inside her skin. Only once she had withdrawn from sight did he turn his attention back to the mood-gauging tapestry on the floor in front of him. He'd never seen such a thing.

Some of the panels were easy enough to figure out. There was an orgy scene, with bodies entwined in the throes of ecstasy. A gentler scene in which a man reclined while a woman read to him. Another scene depicted people eating from a table covered in delicacies. A bathing scene. A sword-fighting scene. Another showing a reclining man being entertained by dancers holding fans. A dozen men and women stood around a table, deep in sombre discussion. A sleeping couple filled another panel. With every step another mood or need satisfied. A man lashed to a wooden X, his back a mass of welts as he writhed beneath the whip. A beautiful woman holding that whip, her expression one of complete control and focus. Punishment delivered, but not in anger, and the man on the cross looked... grateful.

His courtesan had returned with tea; he could hear her off to one side and see her in his peripheral vision.

'You do all this?' he asked, keeping his gaze fixed on the whipping scene. 'Put a man to the lash and strip the guilt from his soul before putting him back together again?' The next scene showed the same woman tending the man's wounds.

'I've been trained to, yes.' She approached from his left and held out a porcelain cup filled with pale amber tea. 'Will you sit?'

He took the tea and let his fingers brush hers. She stilled, and so did he.

He didn't believe in instant attraction. He'd never been a slave to his body's baser demands. But if one tiny touch could send this much heat and awareness coursing through him, imagine what she could do with full body contact?

'It's a trap,' he said at last.

'How so?' Her gaze was steady, her features as smooth as marble.

He gestured towards the depictions of service laid out before him, and it was all very tempting, except that beneath the surface pleasures lay a darker truth altogether. Mind, body and soul. She wasn't here to serve. She was here to own him. 'What wife could ever compete if I had this at my disposal? Where else would I go but here, where every whim would be served up to me on a gilded plate? By the time I'd satisfied every corrupt thought lying dormant in my soul it would be too late for either of us to escape. I'd *own* you, in ways you've never dreamed of. And you'd own me.'

'Well, that's one interpretation,' she said. 'There are others.'

'Tell me some others.'

'Ignore the sexual element and take advantage of my political prowess instead. Arun is a stabilising force in this region. Many would like to keep it that way, including those I answer to. Including you.'

'Am I not doing that already?' Because he thought he was.

'Your plans to unify water resources across four neighbouring nations haven't gone unnoticed. This region will grow to become a power bloc—provided you can hold it together.'

He had Theo, Casimir and Valentine right there with him, a shared vision for their region. 'I can hold it together.'

'Indeed, we think so,' she said. 'But who will explain your ambitions to a wider world that might fear such a power shift?'

'And I suppose you can help me there.'

She couldn't fail to pick up on the sarcasm in his voice but she paid no heed to it. 'The Order of the Kite has contacts you don't yet have. I can make introductions, facilitate communication channels that you will then keep open when I leave.'

'And what's in it for you?'

A tiny smile graced her lips. 'World peace?'

'You're a saint,' he said. 'But I still want to know—what's in it for you personally? I don't understand why a modern-minded woman with your kind of looks and education would choose such a role. I don't know what your angle is. Do you want to marry a man of power and gain power and status through him? What happens after me? Do they send you onto the next visionary King in need? And the next after that?'

'I only need to do this once,' she replied quietly. 'I serve you until you release me, at which point my debt will have been repaid. Then I'm free to choose my own way.'

'What debt?'

'The Order cared for my mother through a long and arduous decline and she died with peace and dignity. They saved me from a life in the gutter.'

'And how old were you when this happened?'

'Does that matter? Others turned away from us. They didn't.'

'It matters.'

A small frown appeared between her eyes. 'I was seven.'

Seven years old and taken and trained and

made to feel beholden to her rescuers. 'So basically you've had no choice but to do what they ask of you.'

'Have you ever had a choice but to serve the monarchy?' she asked, and he glared at her. 'I think not. We are not so different, you and I. You were born into service. In a way, so was I.'

Except that for her it wasn't a lifetime commitment. 'I'm releasing you from your duty. Soon as I can.'

She nodded. 'I'd like that. But at least make use of me first.'

His gaze slid to that cursed wheel of desire on the floor.

'You don't have to take advantage of all that's on offer.' She barely knew him and already she was reading him like a book. That didn't happen to Augustus. Ever. 'But you could take advantage of some of it without surrendering your mortal soul.'

'There's an opening on my staff for a social secretary. I need someone to organise a ball and other smaller events.' He handed the teacup back to her, still full. Not a drop had passed his lips. 'Can we start with that?'

Sera nodded as she set the tea aside. 'Of course.'

'I think fixed boundaries between us would

be best. Meanwhile, is there something I can do to make your stay here more comfortable? Anything you need that you haven't already seen to?' She wasn't a sorceress. He wasn't a lovesick fool, but he could still offer common courtesy.

'If you and I are to be observing fixed boundaries, there is something I'd like to discuss.'

He waited.

It was the first time he'd ever seen her looking nervous.

'Am I free to seek sexual satisfaction elsewhere?'

Continued silence was often a tactic he used to force the other person to speak. This time, pure shock stilled his lips.

Sera of the High Reaches squared her delicate shoulders and fixed him with pleading kitten eyes. 'I've never truly been intimate with another person. That was reserved for you. I'd be lying if I said I wasn't looking forward to it. And seeing you're not of a mind to...'

He wasn't a complete stranger to women becoming impatient for sexual experience. His sister, dear Lord, had been quite adamant about partying up a storm at one point. But not under his roof, and she'd never actually gone through with it. Theo had seen to that, with Augustus's full blessing. Now this.

'You're a *virgin* courtesan?'

'Yes. Do you seriously think they would send someone *used*?'

'Oh, pardon my ignorance. Forgive me that I assumed some small measure of *experience* from a trained *courtesan*!' Never mind the beast in his belly that flicked a scaly tail and roared because she'd been kept pure so that *he* could be her teacher. It wasn't *right* for him to want that, and it certainly wasn't right that she'd had no say in her own sexual enlightenment.

He had a courtesan. A virgin courtesan. Standing there beneath the dome, her midriff bare, hair pulled back and no make-up on her face. 'Do you have someone in mind to be intimate with?'

He had the sudden reckless desire to strangle them.

'I had you in mind,' she said as her gaze briefly dropped to his lips. 'I do know what to do in theory.'

'Theory isn't *doing*. What if I wanted to use you roughly? Tie you down, take away all your control and self-respect and make you beg for release? Take away your ability to reason? Take every slight ever dealt me and transfer them to your flesh? Did your illustrious tutors ever teach you how to deal with sadistic madmen?'

She had no answer for him.

'You know *nothing*,' he challenged.

Her first kiss was his if he wanted it, not to mention the second. All of it. He headed for the door before he lost his mind and took what she offered so freely. He had his hand on the door before something made him look back. She'd fallen to a curtsey facing him and the door, her body placed right in the centre of that cursed carpet depicting every sin and pleasure known to man.

'Get up.' He didn't want this. He didn't dare take it. 'Come here.'

He waited until she stood before him, her eyes betraying uncertainty as he leaned down until their lips almost touched. 'Lord knows I didn't ask for you, but you've come here labelled as *my* courtesan and I will cut the hand off anyone who touches you. No kissing. No sex. No flirting with any of my employees. Are we clear?'

'Clear. Very clear,' she whispered with a tell-tale tremor in her voice. He was scaring her.

And then he got caught in the whirling vortex of her expressive grey eyes, and maybe he wasn't scaring her at all. Because that look right there looked a whole lot like surrender.

'Do the work I ask of you,' he grated. 'Put me in contact with the power brokers you think I need to cultivate. Find me a suitable wife if you can.' He could claim those perfect lips if he wanted to, tease the bow of the upper one with the tip of his tongue, slide in easy and experienced and lay her mouth to waste. She wasn't unwilling. She definitely wasn't unwilling.

'Above all...don't tempt me.'

Sera shut the door behind him and leaned against it, still reeling beneath the weight of his words and that brief brush of his lips against hers. It had barely qualified as a kiss but she could still feel the burn of his palm against her chin and the rough stroke of his thumb against her cheekbone. His breath caressing her lips and the swift charge of desire when their eyes caught and held.

She'd wanted him to kiss her properly. Lay claim or lay to waste; either would have been acceptable. She slid to the floor, both hands between her legs, pressing down hard against the feelings he'd ignited inside her. She was so ready for a physical awakening. All the theory in the world and exploration with her own hands could only get her so far. She wanted *his* hands where her hands were, driving her higher until she broke all over him.

It wouldn't have to be all give on her part and all take on his, even if she did want to read and respond to every nuanced muscle twitch he made. She *had* been trained to please, no matter what he might think. The physical arrangement between courtesan and King didn't have to be the bad thing he was making it out to be. Did it?

Closing her eyes, she pressed up into her hand, seeking release, sharp and swift, as she allowed herself to imagine his kiss. Not the tease he'd left her with.

A proper kiss.

She ran her tongue over the spot where his lips had just been and came moments later, imagining it.

CHAPTER THREE

IT TOOK SERA two days to organise the mid-winter ball. The guest list had already been prepared by Moriana, formerly of Arun and now Queen Consort to the King of Liesend-aach. Her Royal Highness Moriana had returned Sera's call promptly and approved the additional guests Sera had put forward for the express purpose of finding Augustus a wife. Invitations had gone out. The palace staff were happy for someone—anyone—to take the helm and direct the preparations. The ball was an annual event and they were well trained and competent.

After that, there was a dinner for twelve to organise, and then an informal supper for thirty in one of the smaller palace libraries. Moriana had phoned Sera about the library event guest list several times already and once to discuss what books would go on display in the library given the handful of historians on the guest list. Moriana had asked if there were any books belonging to the courtesans of the High Reaches that Sera could put on display.

At that, Sera had hesitated. Some books could be displayed without controversy, but not all. The journals of the courtesans of old were fascinating, but they weren't for public viewing.

Augustus had not been back. No other visitors had called on her and her guards had been incorporated into the regular ranks of the palace, although she still met with them for morning exercise. They met in the horse yard behind the stables, where the sawdust on the ground was sweet and soft. They'd thought it out of the way enough that they wouldn't bother anyone. Three days in and already they had a growing audience for the martial arts patterns they completed in unison and the sparring that came afterwards. Give it another week and the requests for lessons would start. She could see the hunger for more in the eyes of those watching. The curiosity, reluctant admiration, and sometimes the heat.

Always the heat.

Aware of the restlessness riding her, Sera pushed her body hard during morning exercise, as comfortable as she could be with the hot eyes of the crowd, the sun weak and watery and a chill in the air that reminded her of the mountains.

When she met the ground for the third time because of inattention, Ari, the guardsman who'd put her there, stepped back and disengaged from their sparring. She wasn't easy to take down, and this time the kick to her sternum would have broken bones if she hadn't deflected the blow at the last minute. Ari had expected far better from her. She wasn't concentrating.

She lay there, eyes closed and reluctant to take a breath because when she did it was going to hurt. She felt rather than saw someone crouch down beside her and, quick as a snake, she clamped her hand around their wrist as they went to touch her torso.

'Easy.'

She opened her eyes to slits and studied the forearm she'd captured. It was tanned and corded with muscle, the hand looked strong and the fingernails blunt. She looked for a face to match the hand but the sun was directly in her line of sight. It wouldn't be Ari or Tun; they knew better than to offer to help her up.

It might be someone from the audience who didn't understand the limits she lived by.

She moved just enough to let the man's body block the sun, the better to see his face.

Augustus.

She took in a breath and pain didn't slice at her. She eased into a sitting position and didn't pass out. Good news.

'You went down pretty hard,' he said gruffly.

'My own fault,' she murmured, and let go of his arm. He had the right to touch her. She could not refuse.

He stood and held out his hand and slowly, carefully, she put her hand in his and let him help her up.

His hand was more calloused than she'd been expecting from a man who did no physical work. Her hand looked tiny clasped in his. His dark eyes showed no emotion.

'Why are you here?' she asked.

'I live here. And when rumour reaches me that half my security force is turning up on their days off to watch the northerners beat the living daylights out of each other I get curious.'

Fair enough. She took back her hand and spared a glance for her guards. Only two were here with her; the third was on duty. Neither stepped forward, although Ari's fingers flickered a message that hopefully only she could read. Had he injured her?

No.

A silent conversation, meant to set her guardsman at ease.

He didn't seem convinced.

'What may we do for you, Your Majesty?'

'Find somewhere else to practise, for starters. You have half my men-at-arms gagging for a glimpse of you. The other half have already seen you fight and now have a new erotic fantasy to be going on with.'

He wasn't being fair. 'Sawdust is soft and the floors in my quarters are too hard for serious sparring. Where else might we practise? We are also open to teaching those of your court who wish to learn the forms and uses they might be put to. Ari is a master. Tun a champion who will soon retreat to the mountains for his final year of meditation before he too becomes a high practitioner of the art.'

'What grade do you hold?'

'I hold my own.'

'You didn't today.'

'I lost focus. If there's some other place you'd rather we practise we'll take it, Your Majesty. We practise daily, together and alone. It's not just exercise. It's a way of life for those who guard the temples of the High Reaches. It's contact and communication. Learning how to read a person's movements. It's non-sexual. Instructional. There's no harm in it,' she said in the face of his continued silence.

He gave Tun and Ari a glare far sharper than any knife. 'Then why are you hurt?'

'I'm wiser in the face of Ari's takedown. It won't happen again.'

'What did the older one say to you with his sign language?'

She hadn't thought he'd been in any position to see that. 'He wanted to know if I was injured.'

'He could have asked.'

'You were there and seeing to me. Discretion was best.'

'Tell them not to use sign language again in front of my men. It breeds suspicion and there's already far too much of that around here because of you and the old ways you've brought with you.'

It was true; the people here continued to see her as *other*. 'People fear what they don't understand.'

'They also fear rare beauty, overt displays of power and influence and those who never stay down, even when beaten. Especially when beaten. Tone it down, Sera, or I'll shut you in your room full of temptation and beautiful things and leave you there.'

'I'm never going to please you, am I? You give me functions to organise and I organise them. I come meekly when called. I've stacked the midwinter ball full of accomplished single women for you to meet. I've set up introductions with people of influence. What else do you want?'

'I want sweet dreams,' he grated. 'I'd prefer them not to be about you. My sister has just flown in. She says she's already been in contact with you by phone. She wants to meet you.'

Sera wasn't ready for guests, sweaty and aching as she was. She wanted to ask more about his dreams. 'I'll need half an hour before I'm properly presentable.'

'You don't have it,' he said, and opened a half-hidden door in the castle wall. 'After you.'

She had sawdust in her hair and on her sleeve and down the leg of her loose cotton trousers. 'Are you always this petty?' she asked, and watched his eyes narrow.

'It's an impromptu visit and my sister schedules herself so tightly that she never has much time,' he countered. 'Believe me, I like spontaneity less than you do but she's here now and you look fine as you are. Through this door and keep walking for a minute or two. After you.'

She stepped inside and kept to a brisk pace. The corridor was narrow but well lit. The next door he bade her to walk through opened into a large sitting room with a wall full of windows overlooking palace gardens. An elegant woman in a tangerine sundress rose from a chair as they entered. Sera took note of her poise and careful smile before dropping to the floor in a curtsey, suddenly light-headed at the piercing pain coming from somewhere near her ribs. Maybe she had taken some damage after all.

'Moriana, meet Lady Sera, Courtesan of the High Reaches,' Augustus said from somewhere beside her. 'Sera, get up.'

'Augustus, she's not a hound,' Moriana protested.

'If I don't tell her to get up she stays down.' Augustus scowled as he bent forward and curled his hand around her upper arm and drew her to her feet. 'You *are* injured. Don't lie to me again.'

'I'm okay.' If he would stop looking at her as if she were a stain on his shoe she might feel less dizzy and disoriented.

'Have I caught you at a bad time?' his elegant, well-mannered sister asked as Sera swayed and tried to find her centre and her balance. Augustus's hand tightened vicelike around her arm. 'I hope Augustus hasn't had you cleaning out the stables.'

'No, Your Highness.'

'I found her engaged in hand-to-hand combat with two of her guards.'

'For exercise,' Sera stressed.

'Find another form of exercise.' His eyes burned black.

'I've been doing martial arts for fifteen years. If you tell me to give it up I will because I'm duty bound to obey you, so here's a thought. Don't ask me to.'

The quiet clearing of a throat reminded Sera that they weren't alone and she bowed her head in shame. She wasn't presentable or amiable enough for guests. 'I can do better,' she offered quietly, and it was a blanket statement that covered a multitude of sins. 'I will do better.'

'Oh, for f—I'm trying to *protect* you.' He turned to his sister. 'She's here. She's all yours. I have other things to do. If she collapses, leave her where she falls.'

'Augustus!'

Sera watched from beneath lowered lashes

as Augustus stalked from the room, leaving thick silence behind him and no even ground to stand on.

'Well, that was...unexpected,' the King's sister said with no little bemusement. 'What *have* you done with my courteous, by-the-book brother?'

'Barely anything.' And wasn't that the truth. 'He doesn't want me here, Your Highness. That's all.' It underscored their every interaction.

'And how old are you?' Augustus's sister asked next.

'Twenty-three.'

'You look about sixteen. Maybe that's what's bothering him.'

Sera couldn't say.

'Are you here of your own free will?'

'I am.' Perhaps this woman, out of everyone here, would understand. 'I undertake my role willingly and with honour.'

'I'm glad to hear it. But it's been over a hundred years since this court has seen a courtesan of the High Reaches. We are, as a rule, a suspicious lot and fiercely independent. How can you serve my brother? What is it you bring?'

'Political backing and access to people of

influence. You saw the additions to the most recent guest list for the library evening?'

'A diplomat, a peacekeeper and a historian from well beyond our northern borders. Not people we usually deal with.'

'Yet their voices are heard elsewhere, where others have concerns over the grand water plans for this region. What better way to begin conversation than with a casual evening of books, fine food and access to one of the monarchs at the heart of those plans?'

'Are you saying that my brother can't find his own way through the political mire?'

'I'm saying that the Order of the Kite has influence far beyond Arun's reckoning, and beyond Liesendaach's too, never mind your husband's dealings. Should your brother ever ask for access to people who can aid him in his vision, he shall receive.'

'And has he asked?'

'No.' There was the not so small matter of his pride, not to mention his innate suspicion. Trust did not come easily to the royals of Arun. 'There's also the issue of your country needing an heir to the throne.'

'I fail to see how a courtesan can help with that.'

'And yet courtesans throughout the centuries have brokered marriages and more. Something is holding your brother back from making a commitment. Once we understand what it is we can address the issue and find someone who can give him what he needs. I can encourage him to explore or even simply to voice those…needs…in a safe and confidential environment.'

The elegant Queen Consort suddenly looked supremely uncomfortable. 'What makes you think my brother has particular needs?'

'The fact that he's not yet married, perhaps?' There was no delicate way to put this. 'Look, everyone explores their inner desires given the right opportunity. My job is to give the man a non-judgemental space to do it in. Some of the preferences of former Kings of Arun have been quite specific.'

Moriana blinked. 'Do I really want to know?'

'There are journals, milady. As a direct member of Arun's royal family, you have the right to view them.'

'May I see them now?'

'Of course. I have some in my quarters.'

'The rumours surrounding your quarters are quite…elaborate.'

'The rumours are true. Would you like to take tea with me there? Your brother has yet to put a cup of mine to his lips but I assure you there's no poison involved. That would be counterproductive.'

'You do know that I can't tell whether you're joking or not?'

Sera smiled. The King's sister stared.

'I'm beginning to realise the extent of my brother's problem,' Moriana said drily. 'Yes, I'd like to see the journals and what you've done with the round room. I'll cancel the rest of my morning engagements.'

'Wonderful.' Sera thought about curtseying again, but the memory of the pain involved gave her pause. She turned and headed for the door instead, opening it for her companion.

'So you've been working with Augustus and his assistant. Have you met our head of house-hold staff yet?'

Sera nodded. 'And the chefs, function waiting staff, and the head gardener.'

'Have you met my father?'

'Only briefly, Your Highness. He came to view the work of the stonemasons. He didn't stay long.

'He tends to leave things to Augustus these days. Do you have family?' Moriana asked.

'No, Your Highness. My mother died in my early teens and I have no brothers or sisters.'

'And your father?'

Sera paused. 'He is unknown to me.'

'It's just…the accord says you are of noble bloodlines.'

'My mother's ancestry,' said Sera. 'The Order traces its bloodlines through the female.'

'How unusual,' murmured the other woman. 'And when you leave here, once Augustus marries and gives the country an heir, what will you do? More courtesan work? Or do you get to become something else then?'

'There are many forks in my road. Some of them lead to high places and some of them don't. I have contacts the world over and a good education. The opportunities available to me after I've discharged my duty here are truly limitless.'

They'd reached the round room doors. Sera opened them and stood back to allow Moriana to enter. Augustus had not cared for the artwork on display or the comforts on offer; he'd barely glanced at them. Perhaps his sister would show more interest.

Moriana stepped inside, her gaze instantly drawn upward towards the sunlit glass dome. 'It's still stunning, that roof. But the sun doesn't always shine in Arun. I grew up here and I should know. Are you warm enough in here?'

'There's oil heating in the side rooms and alcoves for when the sun doesn't shine and warm the stone in the central dome. It's enough.'

'And far too big for just one person,' murmured Moriana. 'In times of old, how many others would have attended you here?'

'Dozens, Your Highness. But the Lady Lianthe will visit on occasion. And others might also venture here, with your brother's permission. Friends and tutors, other members of the Order.'

'How many members of the Order are there?'

'That I couldn't say. But I'll show you where the journals are. By your leave, I'll make myself presentable while you look at them.' Sera was very aware of the sweat on her skin and the sawdust still clinging to her trousers.

Moriana nodded. 'Shall I ring for tea?'

'I don't ring for service, Your High—'

'Call me Moriana.'

'I don't ring for service, Lady Moriana. I'm the one who serves.'

'Then we shall both serve ourselves,' said Moriana easily. 'You get clean; I'll make the tea. Shall I sit in the middle of the room once I've explored the art on the walls and discovered your journals? Is that appropriate?'

'Of course. The journals are in the glass case in the library alcove. They can't leave here, nor can they be copied. You'll understand why once you begin to read them. Of the other books in the library, I've left some on the table that might be suitable to place on display in the palace reading rooms and libraries. I haven't forgotten your earlier request.'

A visitor, finally, and an important one. Sera shed her clothes and combed out her hair. Not as swiftly as she would have liked, but it couldn't be helped given the state of her ribs. Nothing broken, no, but there was bruising already and had she been alone she'd have iced the area. As it was, she took a soft cotton scarf and wrapped her torso tightly and wished for painkillers. Maybe she'd find some later, but right now she had Moriana of Liesendaach to make welcome.

Sera chose a simple linen tunic and stretchy leggings to wear over her makeshift bandage. Loose enough to hide the torso wrap, embroidered enough to show her respect. She wound her hair into a bun, slipped her feet into backless high heeled sandals and swiftly applied eyeliner, mascara and soft, moist lipstick.

By the time Sera returned, almost ten minutes later, Moriana was standing at the edge of the floor tapestry that had so captivated Augustus, a fragile porcelain cup in her hand.

'This is quite something,' she said as Sera approached. 'Does it tell a story?'

'It's a request wheel, my Lady Moriana. You arrive and sit where you will, according to need, and I will see to that need.'

Moriana froze, her cup of tea halfway to her lips.

'Your brother doesn't like it,' Sera added. 'I think he found the whipping scene somewhat confronting.'

'Uh-huh,' his well-spoken sister said with a blush. 'So he's supposed to come in and choose his…'

'Fix,' suggested Sera. 'Yes. Having said that, he's been here exactly once and refused a seat. Perhaps he just needs to get used to it. It saves quite a lot of time.'

'Uh-huh.' No more tea for Lady Moriana. She returned her cup to the saucer she held in her other hand and walked a slow, rapt circle around the tapestry. 'There's an orgy scene.'

'Yes. If you don't mind me saying so, you Arunians do seem a little repressed.'

Moriana smiled faintly. 'Perhaps. Do you have a favourite scene?'

'I like reading aloud to people.' She'd

learned that particular skill while tending to the children of the High Reaches. 'I like spirited intellectual debate and reasoned argument, so I quite like the conversation scenes too. As for the sex scenes…' Chances were she'd like those too if she ever got a chance to indulge in them. 'Each to his own, no?'

Moriana hadn't yet fled the room screaming. This was a good thing. 'What's the one with the people standing around the table covered with maps?'

'Strategy sessions for weighty subjects like war and succession. There is a book to accompany the carpet. I've set it aside for your brother, assuming he ever wants to see it.'

'I could take it to him when I leave here,' Moriana offered. 'It might be better presented to him as a curious artefact rather than a working guide to your services.'

Sera nodded. 'Please do. Would you like to sit?'

'This…circle…works for me too?'

'Of course.'

'So if I wanted to sit and discuss my brother's marriage options with you, which panel would I choose?'

'You might choose the panel with the maps. Strategy session,' Sera offered. 'I'd get my computer and take a seat within that area also and we'd discuss options. I'd provide refreshments. More tea or cold drinks, stuffed dates or something savoury. We'd plot and plan and consider what we already know when it comes to the monarchy's needs and preferences. We'd come up with a list I would then consult whenever I have to plan another function or dinner and I would make sure to get the women on that list in front of him.'

Moriana sat where suggested and the world did not end. She took a deep breath and then looked up at Sera with a smile. 'I love stuffed dates.'

'Tell me…' Sera was wholly prepared to woo the King's sister to within an inch of her life. 'Do you like them dipped in chocolate?'

CHAPTER FOUR

IT WAS A TRAP. Even as Augustus stood at the door to Sera's quarters at half eight the following evening and pulled on the bell to signal his presence, he knew he should have stayed away or at the very least had her brought to his office earlier in the day. He wanted to talk about this list of potential brides she and Moriana had cooked up between them. The first three on the list would be presented to him at the Winter Solstice ball, Moriana had said. Sera would not be present.

What good was a matchmaker if she wasn't even going to be present?

The door in front of him opened, and this time the menace from the High Reaches stood ready to serve him. He'd told her he was coming. He'd given her a time frame and ample opportunity to get ready for him. Nothing was going to happen except conversation. Moriana had navigated that blasted courtesan's carpet wheel successfully enough, and there was even a training manual to go with it. He'd browsed through it during his lunch break.

He was getting more used to the physical effect Sera of the High Reaches seemed to have on him. Eyes soft and inviting, lips curved in welcome. Her over-tunic a flowing drape of gossamer moss-coloured silk, then underneath a plum-coloured bodice and straight skirt that finished an inch or so below the tunic. Her hair had been pulled back into a high ponytail yet still reached her waist. Delicate silver fans with tassels fell from her ears and swung gently as she moved. Matching tassels fell from the place where she'd gathered her hair. Her make-up was subtle rather than overwhelming.

She was breathtaking.

Wordlessly, she invited him to enter and he did.

'May I take your jacket?' she asked. He thought *Why not?* and let her ease it from his shoulders and hang it on a wooden clothes dummy in the alcove beside the door. She closed the door behind him and studied his face intently. 'I haven't curtseyed,' she said.

And for that he was grateful. Every time she did she fed a demon that demanded he take ad-

vantage of her willingness to grant him anything he wanted. 'How are your ribs?'

'Perfectly fine, thank you.'

There was a new table in the round room.
A small round table with room enough for
three people to sit around comfortably or four
people at a squeeze. There was a new sofa as
well, although the round one and the cursed
floor tapestry still took pride of place. This
new sofa had been placed against a wall. A
stack of reading books sat next to it and two
wing-back leather library chairs had been positioned to either side. The carpet in between
looked thick and plush and was a deep and
solid red. She saw him looking at the set-up
and extended a graceful arm in its direction.

'I took the liberty of setting up another seat-
ing area. Your sister thought it might encourage more visitors, or, at the very least, make
them less suspicious once they got here.'

His sister was a genius when it came to putting people at ease.

'You must miss her,' Sera said next.

'We all do.' He'd once thought Moriana neu-
rotic and highly strung. He'd thought his palace would run just as smoothly without her
incessant attention to detail. It hadn't. A fact
which had surprised him and approximately no

one else in the palace. 'My sister used to manage the monarchy's social obligations. There can be two or sometimes even three social functions a day here. And then there are the balls and state dinners. She left comprehensive instructions for every event, but even so I miss her judgement when it comes to who to seat where and what alliances are to be encouraged. It's all in her head, and in mine, and neither of us have time to download a lifetime's worth of observations into someone else's brain. Especially when that someone is just as likely to go to the press with tasty gossip at the first opportunity.' He was tired and irritable and what was it about this woman that had him spilling confidences like an overwrought teenager?

Moving on.

Moriana had sat in the strategy section yesterday morning, she'd told him. It had worked for her. It would work for him. He strode to the central sofa and sat in the area with the people and the table and the maps. Strategy session.

Sera smiled at him, really smiled, as if he'd made her happy, and—oh, *crap*.

Could he order her not to smile at him like that?

'Would you like water, wine, coffee or tea?' she asked.

'None of it. Go get the list of potential wives you and my sister cooked up between you and then take a seat. I have some amendments to make.' He hoped he sounded rigidly officious rather than downright surly but he didn't like his chances. Neither option was a good example of confident, competent leadership.

'I'll get my computer,' she said, and when she came back she sat beside him easy as you please and earnest in her role as matchmaker. For his part, he found himself moving closer, well and truly enmeshed by her delicate perfume and perfect profile and the little fan earrings that brushed the skin of her neck.

All of it was captivating and it took all the willpower he had to turn his attention to the database full of potential brides. A database full of not just names but lineages, occupations, hobbies and… 'Is that a character assessment column?'

'Subjective, of course, and predominantly based on their public personas. They may be quite different underneath. We can adjust it as we go. It would be helpful if you could give me some indication as to what you admire most in a woman,' she said. 'Do you want someone with a calm disposition or are you after more fire than that? Someone fun-loving and easy-going or someone more highly strung and demanding? A pliable companion or someone you might on occasion have to work to placate?'

'Meekness bores me. Theatrics annoy me. And stupidity is an unpardonable sin.'

Sera's fingers flew across the keyboard and several names disappeared. 'Any hair, eye or skin colour preferences?'

'None.' He hadn't known he had a preference for grey eyes, raven-dark hair and skin the colour of pale rose petals until a few days ago. Hopefully his current obsession would be short-lived.

'Will you entertain marriage to a woman whose religion is different to yours?' she asked.

'No. She would have to convert.' The demands of the Crown overrode all else in that regard.

More names disappeared from the list.

'Would you like a virgin?' she asked.

'Are you serious?'

Her fingers paused over the keyboard. 'Ah… yes? Historically—'

'Let's keep it modern day.'

'The question stands,' she offered quietly. 'Some things are best left to those who enjoy initiating others. Do you want a virgin or would you prefer someone who brings adequate experience to sexual matters?'

'It's not important!' Said no scaly possessive alpha beast ever.

'Okay.' Another pause. 'Thank you for answering.'

'You're blushing,' he told her darkly. 'All virgin brides aside, how can you possibly think yourself ready to do some of the things in these pictures when you've never been touched?'

His virgin courtesan. The idea was ridiculous.

Beyond ridiculous.

No wonder it kept him awake at night.

'Bodies can be prepared in advance for just about anything. It's the endorphins.' Sera stared at the screen, delicate colour still filling her cheeks. 'More specifically, increased levels of oxytocin can act as a natural pain inhibitor. Additionally, minds can be manipulated to respond with pleasure to dominance, submission or many other…things.'

All of a sudden the idea of a virgin concubine wasn't ridiculous at all, and it was burning hot in this room built for pleasure. 'So you think you're ready for anything?'

'I hope I am. To be otherwise would be unacceptable. Disgraceful.'

'On what planet is not being ready to partake in an orgy or whip a man bloody disgraceful?' She had a flawless knack for rousing his temper. 'Dammit, Sera. I have no idea who you're answering to!'

'I answer to you.'

'The hell you do! Otherwise you'd be gone from here, as requested! Do you even understand the Pandora's box of problems you bring with you? That I'm trying to *work* through while keeping you protected?'

'I don't need protecting.'

'You say you're innocent. The innocent *always* need protecting.' He stood abruptly and stepped away from temptation before he did something unforgivable. 'Read out the remaining names,' he ordered, and she did, her voice becoming steadier as she went. He had her remove several more names from the list, because he'd met those women before and they weren't for him. He found himself circling the sofa, and then moving further afield, looking at other tapestries and sculptures, other furniture sent to grace a courtesan's workplace.

Over and over, his feet returned him to the centre of the room where she sat, his gaze drawn to the pleasure wheel at her feet. Where would a virgin trained as a courtesan even want to start when it came to serving someone sexually?

Finally the names stopped coming and his reason for being there ended.

'It would help if you could give me some additional ideas of what you're looking for in a wife,' she said.

Good question, but he didn't really have an answer for himself, let alone one he'd ever voiced to anyone else. He was so used to *not* voicing his innermost thoughts. 'Why? So you can sell a list of my private wants and needs to the highest bidder?'

'I would never do that. No courtesan of the High Reaches would ever betray your confidence. Above all else, it is the rule that governs us.'

He wanted to believe her. And really, what would it matter if people knew what he was looking for in a wife? The basics, at any rate.

'Resilience is important,' he offered, and wondered why it was easier to talk to her than just about anyone. 'There's no point choosing a wife who'll crumble beneath the pressures and constrictions placed on her. She'll be bound by duty to Crown and country. She'll have to cope with extensive press coverage wherever she goes. I want her at the centre of things, right by my side, and she needs to be stubborn and curious, observant, intuitive and good with people she barely knows.'

Now that he'd started, he didn't know how to stop confiding in her, because he *had* thought about this. He'd thought about this long and hard and it was good to finally say some of it out loud. 'Above all I want to know what's going to keep her at my side when the going gets tough. Because it will. My mother loved my father above all else and he loved her. This country benefitted greatly from their love match. My sister loves Theo and he loves her. Liesendaach wins. Sometimes I doubt I have the capacity to *be* in love with another person in that same way. And yet I can see the benefits. The strength in it. I'm not against it.'

Too much.

Too much revealed.

He turned away to study yet another tapestry that hung on a nearby wall. She had no comment for him other than the tapping of computer keys.

'Okay,' she said finally. 'And, forgive me the intrusion, but do you find sex satisfactory?'

'What are you now? My virgin sex therapist?'

'Do you need one?'

He barked a laugh. Better than a growl for this confidante with a sharply honed wit. 'I get by.'

'Some of your ancestors have preferred men. They've required wives who could accommodate those preferences. Turn a blind eye at times.'

'I prefer women.' Truth.

'What of fidelity?' she asked. 'Will you practise it?'

'Yes.'

'Do you require fidelity from your wife?'

'Yes.' Surely she knew this already? He'd already banned her from taking her kisses elsewhere and had almost punished her guard the other morning for daring to spar with her. 'I don't share.'

More typing and no comment whatsoever.

'I'm thirty years old. I prefer women to men. I've never been in love. And I thought I had more time in which to marry before the courtesans of old descended from a mystical mountain to help me do my duty,' he offered curtly. 'I can find my own wife, regardless of what you, your Order or my sister might think. The only reason I'm here is because I refuse to let you conspire behind my back. You may as well conspire with me. It'll go much faster if we work together on this.'

'Yes, I know,' she offered quietly.

'I also want to be able to explain your role here without calling into question my sanity, my morals or yours. From here on in when you're dealing with my staff or handling guest lists you'll be known as Lady Sera Boreas, Executive Function Manager for the Royal Palace of Arun. You'll answer to me or my executive secretary. You will oversee the functions in person but not be in attendance as a guest. I want you in corporate clothing. Smart suits, modest jewellery, tidy hair. No shackles or manacles, no golden bustiers, no six-inch heels while you're on duty in public.'

'And in private?'

'I can't tell you what to do once you're in the privacy of your own quarters.'

'Actually, you ca—'

'Don't say those words.'

It occurred to him that he was already telling her what to do in the privacy of her quarters, and he smiled without humour. It was an impossible situation and he saw no way out of it other than to make her leave or turn her into a respectable employee of the palace. He waved his hand around the room. 'All that you've brought to my palace works against me in the wider world. The rebirth of these quarters is all my staff can talk about. Word has spread. King Augustus of Arun keeps a courtesan hidden in a round room, built like a birdcage. He's been bewitched, his needs are dark, he's not a modern-day king. You're a sorceress, a temptress, a creature of myth. That's what they're saying about you, me and this situation. It's time to take control of this narrative.'

'You want to reframe me.'

He nodded. 'Minimise the mystery. Modernise the mythology. I need you to arrange for one piece of art to be displayed in the palace's grand entrance hall. I want notes to accompany it, emphasising its historical significance. I want a dozen books from your collection showcased in the state library, several pieces of art or treasures of historical significance in circulation throughout our galleries. I want a narrative built around the Order of the Kite that starts with it being supportive, historically complex, non-political, culturally significant and ends with the information about your current non-sexual role in my administration. I want you to give history talks in university lecture halls and libraries. I want you to be the guest of honour as each treasure on display is unveiled. I want you to talk about the Order of old and then I want you to talk about the roles women have traditionally played in government, the roles open to them today and your own education.'

'Your Majesty, the Order does *not* seek publicity.'

'Then they shouldn't have sent you here.' His gaze clashed with hers, storm clouds meeting a bleak black sea. 'I'm asking you to be a modern-day woman for a modern-day audience. One who embraces the history and power of your Order and can competently explain your presence here. One who shines a favourable light on us both. Do it or I'll do it for you.'

Augustus shoved his hands in his pockets and turned away. Looking at her never ended well. He always grew resentful of his body's instinctive response and his brain lost its way. 'You're not stupid, Sera. Philosophy, politics and economics—those are your degree subjects and you only ever earned distinction marks or higher. If you want power here I'm challenging you to take it openly. Carve out a place for yourself that the public will accept. That *I* can accept.' He spared a glance for the pleasure wheel. 'Because there are too many elements here that I *dare* not accept.'

'Your Majesty—'

He wanted to hear her say his name. Not *Your Majesty* or *milord* or *sire*. Only his mother and sometimes his sister had managed to make his name sound anything more than an unwieldy mouthful. They'd laced it with affection and love. Exasperation too, for his cool and calculating deliberations. His father didn't call him by name all that often. His father called him *Son* and it was a reminder of his role in the continuation of their line more than anything.

He wanted to hear her say his name but there was no picture in the carpet for that. 'The only words I want to hear out of your mouth are "I accept your challenge and this amazing opportunity to become a relevant member of your court".'

Silence filled the room as he looked up to the soaring ceiling, anywhere but at the woman seated somewhere to his left. There were other ways he could deal with this. Send her away on a quest, take his case to parliament and the high courts and dissolve the accord and make an enemy of a secret Order with tentacles everywhere. The way he'd outlined— dealing openly with a modern interpretation of her position here—was by far the best. But he needed her co-operation.

'I accept your challenge.'

He closed his eyes as her soft words slid through him and with them came relief. 'Your owls have returned,' he said by way of acknowledgement. 'Two of them. Are they inside or out?'

'In. But I don't think they've returned. I think these ones were merely absent when Tomas came for the rest. I'm glad they were both away and not just one of them. I think they're a mated pair.'

'Do you know what kind they are?'

'Tomas tells me they're Great Horned Owls. I sent him photos. Lianthe would say it's a good omen.'

'And what do you say?'

'As long as they stay up there and I stay down here, I say we can probably come to some kind of mutual living arrangement. The bathing pool was filled today.' It was a change of topic, a change of voice—lighter now, with a faint undercurrent of enthusiasm. He risked a backwards glance and found her standing and somehow changed. More hopeful, perhaps. More relaxed. 'It really has been a pleasure to see this place come alive again. It's been over a hundred and twenty years since anyone's lived here. Don't you find that just a little bit fascinating?'

Memory conjured up the marble pool room, with fancy tiles, private alcoves and exposed stone benches. He did want to see the transformation; there was no denying it. 'Show me.'

The dirty grey colours he remembered now glowed ivory, each marble vein shining beneath layers of polish. Sera flicked a switch and lit the area, contemporary lighting, all of it, but it felt as if flame flickered and shadows danced.

'What are the alcoves full of pillows for?' he asked.

'Massage, body treatments, sex. There's a steam room here too. I know you'll not use any of it but we went with authenticity. This was its function.'

She had such an easy way of saying *sex*. As if it was nothing. Just another function of the body. He'd never found it so, endorphins or otherwise. Sex was revealing, and he far preferred to keep his own counsel. 'And the main pool is heated?'

'To three degrees above body temperature. Three hundred years ago your forebears and mine used fire to heat the pool. Yesterday, engineers from the High Reaches laid solar strips to the framework of the dome. This part of your palace now powers itself, and then some.'

Her face had lit up and her pleasure at the improvements seemed real.

He'd agreed to modifications to the rooms Sera occupied. He hadn't specifically agreed to *any* of this. Under the guise of honouring tradition, it felt as if the power here had been quite deftly wrested from his grasp.

She watched him from the shadows while he struggled with what to do with her in private as well as in public.

'Would you like to bathe?' she asked at last—she had to know he wanted more than that. She'd been taught to read people, had she not? Surely she could see the tension and the want in him and not just for warm water. He wanted what the cursed pleasure wheel had told him he could have. He wanted her hands on him, undressing him, washing his hair as he reclined. All those things the bathing picture showed and more, while the light from the wall sconces threw puppet shadows on the walls.

'I shouldn't.'

'Seems a shame to let it go to waste.'

'Don't tempt me.'

'Sometimes a bath can be just a bath.'

'Say my name.' He needed to hear it fall from those perfect lips.

She looked at him, as if trying to read his mood and good luck with that.

'That was an order.'

'Augustus.'

She made it sound like welcome and desire all rolled into one and he tried not to curse as he shoved his hand through his hair and tried to make sense of both his demands and his resistance. 'Did they make you practise that?'

They had. Sera knew better than many how to modulate her voice to convey different feelings. But the breathlessness in her voice this time was all hers. She gestured towards a stack of towels and potions, trying to get back on track. 'Augustus, would you like to bathe? The pool is ready and I've had lessons in how to make the experience a relaxing one. I could wash your hair. Oils to soothe, invigorate and everything in between. What is your mood?'

'You mean you can't tell?'

'You're hard to read.' She hadn't been expecting the way forward for her that he'd proposed. A public image to craft and shape. A role beyond those already identified by the tapestry. And nothing but strict hands-off in private. It was the keeping-distance-in-private request she would have the most trouble with. 'Or you could bathe alone and I can go and read a book in another room. This pool is for *your* use, Augustus. In any way you see fit.'

She turned away, left him to his thoughts, and approached a small side table groaning with essential oils and liquid soaps. She reached for the sandalwood, bergamot and orange and mixed them in a hand bowl, taking her time. 'I find ritual soothing,' she murmured, still not looking at him as she took the bowl to the water's edge and poured the fragrant oil mix into it, rinsing the bowl three times before setting it aside and rising. 'But if you prefer less ritual and more distance, perhaps you might cast me in the role of pool attendant. I can pile towels by the side of the pool and leave you to it.'

She didn't want to shatter the fragile peace they'd created this evening. She wanted it to continue.

'What does the ritual involve?' he rasped.

'I would remove your clothes, provide your soap, wash your hair, towel you dry, moisturise your skin and dress you again. It can take up to an hour of your time.'

'And what's in it for you?'

'Ritual soothes me. And also…'

'Also what?'

'You're not going to like it.' He wasn't going

to *accept* it. 'I want to serve here, the way I've been trained to serve. It doesn't have to be sexual. It doesn't have to be complicated. You could find refuge and relaxation here if you wanted to.'

'Do it.'

His words didn't come from a place of acceptance. They came at her twisted and wrapped in loathing. Not a good start but at least she had permission to try to bathe him properly.

She ventured closer, until she was standing in front of him. Undressing a man wasn't a hard thing to do. There was an order to the releasing of buttons and the removal of clothes. She knew what to do. Only her trembling fingertips betrayed her as she reached for one of his wrists, turned his forearm towards her and fumbled with the tiny cufflink there. She bit her lip, intent on her task, and wondered if the crazy throb of the pulse point at his wrist was for her.

She slowed her breathing and got on with her task, undoing first one cufflink and then the other. She stepped in closer as she undid his tie, and his eyes never left her face and hers never left his. Buttons, so many buttons on his shirt, tracking a path down his chest, the last of them hidden beneath his trousers as she pulled the shirt free and dealt with them too. Buttons and knuckles and air that had suddenly grown too thin for breathing.

'This isn't going to end well,' he rasped.

'Relax. I'm a professional.' She pushed the front of his shirt aside and slid her hands up and over his shoulders, taking his shirt with her. By the time she'd smoothed her hands down his arms the shirt was on the floor.

She knelt at his feet, removing his shoes and socks and running her hands up his legs and over his thighs as if soothing a savage beast. She kept her hands on him as she undid his trousers, slid her hands beneath his waistband and down over his buttocks, taking the fabric with her, all the way down his legs. 'Put your hand on my shoulder or my head for balance,' she said, as she lifted first one foot from the puddle of his trousers and then the next.

His boxers were stretched tight over his manhood, plumper now than it had been moments ago but not yet at full stretch. If she removed his underwear in the same manner she'd removed his trousers she was going to get an eyeful.

And then she leaned in, her hands high on his thighs, and breathed him in.

Hours of video instruction had done nothing to prepare Sera for the impact of the man standing before her. The heat coming from his skin and the scent of him. The glittering black eyes and his complete attention.

She didn't know where or how he exercised but he did, his body lean and his belly ridged with muscle. He had body hair but not a lot. His manhood looked thick beneath the thin stretch of cotton, and she wondered if her mouth would fit around it. Not just thick but long as well. The stretch for her mouth and throat would be considerable.

He took a ragged breath and stepped away from her touch and shed his boxers. He was beautiful naked. He was beautiful everywhere.

'I'll take that bath now.' His voice whispered over her, making promises not kept by his retreating body. She felt the loss of his regard as he stepped into the water and submerged himself completely. The bathing rituals went unobserved as she knelt on a cushion and waited for him to need something more from her, hands clasped in her lap, back straight, head bowed. Still and silent until needed. Ritual.

She watched from beneath her lashes as he selected soap and started washing, his touch far rougher than hers would have been. She

watched him rinse off, water running in rivu-
lets down the hard planes of his chest, dripping
from his elbows as he pushed dark tendrils
of hair away from his face. He caught her
watching him and stilled. Did he want to get
out now? Should she anticipate his need for a
towel? Would he accept one from her hand?
Bathing rituals shot to hell by him, leaving her
untethered and wanting.

'Sera.'

Surely she could look her fill now that he'd
called her name. She lifted her head.

'Will you wash my hair?'

Finally, something she had previous experience with. She almost fell over herself in her
haste to fetch the water jug and shampoo selection. Ritual, as he watched her prepare the
edge of the pool and gesture for him to lie back
with his head in the shallow dip. She leaned
over and filled the jug, wetting his hair all over
again, her hand firm on his forehead to prevent
water trickling down his face.

She opted for a firmer touch than the one
she'd used on the children of the High Reaches,
massaging his scalp once the conditioner had
gone on and drawing from him a groan that
made her smile her relief.

'Harder,' he rasped, so she increased the

pressure from her fingertips and leaned into it. With his eyes closed she could study his profile more closely. Inevitably, her gaze moved on from his lips to his chest, then his stomach and onto lower depths. His legs were slightly parted. His manhood looked erect.

When she finally turned her attention back to his face, he was watching her through narrowed eyes.

Hot-faced, she filled the water jug again and began to rinse his hair.

He let her finish, he gave her that, and then he was underwater again, and again, and then standing and heading for the steps.

To ogle his sharply defined muscles and the proud jut of his arousal or pick up a towel and have it ready for him? Sera knew what she ought to be doing. She'd trained for this.

By the time she reached the side of the pool and handed him a towel and he'd taken it and wiped his face and dropped it and stood naked before her, she met his gaze unflinchingly. He had nothing to be ashamed of.

Neither did she.

'If you could kiss me in one place and one place only, where would you kiss?' he demanded.

She'd seen so much sex in the guise of instruction. She knew the psychology and physiology behind each and every action, but knowing wasn't doing and she'd never done any of it. His lips beckoned, the fierce cut of his cheekbones. The curve of his shoulder appealed, the water droplet sliding down his neck—she could lap it up and find the pulse point.

But his hand moved to curl around his erection and it drew her gaze like a lodestone. More than anything else, she wanted to know more of *that*. For some reason, kissing his lips seemed like more of an intrusion than kissing him *there*.

He looked so good naked and wanting, almost vibrating with tension as he waited for her to choose which part of him to kiss. He might not even allow it. Maybe all he wanted to know was her preference so he could destroy her with wanting and never having any of it.

She dropped to her knees and his eyes flared a heated warning.

'Really?' he rasped.

'I want to know what it's like,' she replied. 'Do you?'

'I already know.'

She kept her gaze on his face, willing him to let her have this. 'I want to know too.'

'Brave,' he rasped. 'Did they teach you how to do this?'

'Yes.' With toys and tutorials but it was nothing compared to the soft warmth of his shaft as she leaned forward and placed her moist and parted lips against the most sensitive area just beneath the tip.

She tongued him carefully and he tasted of nothing but water. Not until she ran her tongue across the slit did she get a sense of his essence. The skin was slick and smooth. His hiss was hopefully one of pleasure. She knew not to use her teeth. She sucked, ever so gently, and received a fresh burst of flavour for her efforts.

'That's it,' he murmured. 'How much can you take?'

All of it. She closed her eyes and opened her throat and took him deep, down to where her lips met his testicles and she had to breathe through her nose. His hand came to cover her head, not pushing, just keeping her there, then he slowly withdrew until only the tip of him touched her lips.

'Breathe,' he ordered, even as his hand reversed its pressure and he drew her back down onto him. 'Again.'

She lost herself in the rhythm of his slow and measured thrusts.

'Put your hands on me,' he said, and she did, first his thighs while her thumbs brushed the swell of his balls, and then more boldly while he simultaneously thrusted and cursed.

'Look at me,' he ordered on his next withdrawal and she opened her eyes while he searched her face as if studying a puzzle he had no answer for. 'You like this,' he muttered finally. 'Heaven help us both.'

Yes, she liked it. The careful thrusting, his innate gentleness and iron control. The satisfaction that came of knowing that she was the cause of his arousal. She knew how to finish a man, theoretically. Suck and swallow, throat muscles working him over, but when she tried he withdrew so fast and roughly he left her blinking up at him. What had she done? Or not done? 'I'm sorry, I—'

'Don't apologise,' he said, but she still felt as if she'd failed and he must have seen some of that thought written on her face, because he groaned and hauled her up and into his arms and crashed his mouth down over hers, hard and hungry, all power and unrestrained passion, and she responded in kind because this kiss was better than anything she'd ever felt.

He groaned into her mouth and she swallowed it down and opened for more. He tilted her head and consumed her and she fisted her hand in his hair and worked her lips down his neck, nipping and sucking, because she could do that to him here, and skating the edge of violence suited her, suited them both.

She had too many clothes on and he had none. They were ignoring so many steps in the sex-making process. Or maybe they weren't.

'Take me in hand,' he muttered. 'Touch me.' He lifted her bodily and she curled her legs around him. He put her back to a column and rocked against her as his mouth claimed hers again.

He came with layers of silk clothing still between them, grinding down hard against her core and tipping her over into orgasm moments after his own release, strong hands to her buttocks, wet hair at odds with the harsh heat of his breath and the still scorching feel of his mouth on hers. She'd always known about the fire deep down inside her. It was the reason they'd chosen her.

She'd suspected from the beginning that there was a matching fire in him.

After a dozen more harsh breaths, both his and hers, he set her gently on her feet and turned away, not looking at her once as he found his clothes, put them on. He didn't speak, didn't look her way as he headed for the main room and swiftly strode towards the door. He didn't speak as he opened it and let himself out. He left, that was all.

And then the emptiness crashed down on her.

CHAPTER FIVE

AUGUSTUS, RULER OF ARUN, had always kept himself tightly under control. Born to inherit his father's throne, raised to think before he spoke, to weigh and qualify every action. His sister had been the unruly one, governed by her emotions, and only careful tutelage and cultivation of a serene public persona had ever contained her. For Augustus it had been easy. Not for him the pitfalls of adolescent crushes or fierce bursts of anger. He was the cool-headed one, the old soul, the stuffy one. No unexpected or unplanned behaviour from Augustus of Arun. He knew what he had to do at all times and he did it, all childhood resistance to his lot in life long since diminished.

So what the ever-loving hell had just happened in there?

Because he'd never done that before in his life. Taken his own pleasure and given nothing back in return. Leave a woman, *any woman*, let alone a virgin, leaning against a wall for support, her clothes stained and her eyes blown wide with shock, her lips...

Her lips...

What she'd done with them.

He could write an incoherent ode to them.

What had he done? Where was all his rigid moral certainty now?

No one should be made to serve the way she had been groomed to serve him. Even kings needed barriers. Free rein and ultimate power was never a good combination. That was how despots were created.

He hadn't even given her pleasure.

Augustus stopped to lean against the cold stone of the corridor wall. He closed his eyes and bowed his head and tried to make sense of what he'd done. He was attracted to Sera—had been from the moment he'd laid eyes on her. He'd wanted to set her free from the duty bestowed on her and he'd tried. He'd combed every old text and obscure law journal he could find for ways to release her. It was the honourable thing to do. So far, so good. And while that was still happening he'd allowed her to settle into those dusty old quarters and revive a tradition long dead, and legitimise it with artwork and furnishings, and he'd left her alone to get on with it. He'd given her a secretarial role to be going on with because he'd needed a social organiser and she'd needed to serve.

He'd let her draw up a list of potential brides, not because he wanted to get married but because if he did marry she would surely go away. A stupid reason to marry but he needed to marry sooner or later and he wasn't complaining.

He'd behaved.

Right up until he hadn't.

He'd left her standing there, wide-eyed and mute, her mouth a wreck and her body trembling.

He heard a slight sound, a shuffle, and opened his eyes and met the shadowy gaze of one of her guards, half hidden in a recess. The man wanted him to know he was there, that much was obvious. Would he check on Sera once Augustus had gone? Would he comfort her and curse his King?

When had all reason and rational good sense deserted him?

Augustus pushed away from the wall and turned back towards the double doors that kept people out and Sera in. He rang the bell and stared at the flowers and waited.

Nothing happened.

He rang the bell again, and this time, after several more impatient seconds, a peephole opened and he moved to stand in front of it.

She opened the door to him in silence, a towel wrapped around her otherwise wet and naked body.

Washing the stench of him away, he thought grimly, and his heart clenched.

'Your Majesty,' she said, and her voice was huskier than it had been earlier, and he certainly knew why.

'You know my name.'

Only she didn't say it.

'May I come in?'

She stood aside and opened the door and glanced behind him and so did Augustus. The guard stood there watching them, fully visible now, arms crossed in front of his chest and his eyes sharp. Augustus didn't know what she did—more of that silent communication business—but the guard nodded slightly and faded from view.

'You told him you had everything under control?' he asked.

'Yes.'

'Is that what you really think?'

'I think you're conflicted.'

'I think I'm a monster,' he said.

'Because you gave me what I asked for?'

'You didn't ask for that.' She looked at him sharply and then glanced towards the big circular sofa. 'I don't want to sit at your cursed wheel,' he muttered. 'You were bathing. Do you need to continue with that?' She might as well be clean. God knew no amount of water was going to wash him clean of this sin.

With the grace of a dancer and no inhibitions whatsoever, she walked towards the pool and shed her towel before stepping lightly into the water, deeper and deeper still, until she was shoulders deep and her hair billowed about her like tendrils of ink.

'I'm sorry.' She'd never know how much. 'The way I treated you earlier was unacceptable.'

She watched him pace and then reached for the soap. 'You fear passion,' she said.

'No.'

She raised an elegant eyebrow.

'I lost control. I took without thinking. I hurt you.' The way she'd taken him in her mouth, letting him push deeper than he'd ever pushed before—all animal instinct. 'I can hear the damage in your voice.'

She looked at him, her thoughts her own,

and then swam to a tap and turned it on and pushed her face beneath it and opened her mouth and drank. He wanted to look away from the innocent abandon in even that small act. The open mouth and the eyes that never stopped watching him, cataloguing every tiny twitch—or so he imagined. She swallowed and so did he, remembering, and the deep ache of desire that should have been sated sputtered to life again.

She swallowed more and then turned the tap off and cleared her throat. 'How do I sound now?'

A little less rough. 'Your lips are still swollen.' The make-up was off but the lush redness remained.

'I can't tell.' She was at the side of the pool again, closest to him, all graceful hands and arms, breasts with the nipples puckered up tight, but she wasn't self-conscious—not one little bit—and he looked away and kept right on pacing, wondering why he'd turned around and come back because he was unravelling all over again. 'Have you finished bathing?' she asked solemnly.

He'd finished undressing in front of her, full-stop. At least one of them should be clothed at all times. It was his new motto when dealing with her. 'I didn't—'

She waited for him to continue.

'You didn't—'

She was still waiting for him to finish a damn sentence.

'First times should involve satisfaction for all concerned,' he muttered finally. 'I should have made it so. I can still show you what it can be like.'

'By taking control?'

'Yes.' By taking control and keeping it and pasting over the last twenty minutes with something infinitely more palatable.

'You do realise that my satisfaction isn't the goal here?' she asked, and that, more than anything else in this crazy set-up, made his temper spike.

'Because your teachers say so? Because you're here to serve and my satisfaction comes before yours? Because you don't deserve a first kiss that's gentle and respectful? Because, believe me, Sera of the High Reaches, everyone deserves that.'

'It wasn't gentle, true.' She was getting out of the bath now and walking towards him, water caressing her skin. 'But my self-respect is intact, even if yours is not.' She tilted her head back to look at him. 'Your ego is bruised because you think I didn't like your taste or touch? I can assure you I did.'

How could she have?

Her eyes seemed to soften as she stared at him. 'Would you like to try again?' she invited softly. 'Bolster your ego, dilute your guilt— whatever it is that brought you back here to apologise? Because you can kiss me again if you like.'

It wasn't *about* him. 'What would *you* like? From me?'

'Right now?'

'Right now.' Because he'd do it. 'This isn't about me.'

'Do you really believe that?' She picked up a towel and patted her face and wrapped it around her small frame and tucked it in. She pushed her hair to one side and combed through it with her fingers before wrapping slender fists around the dark mass and stripping the water from it in one smooth movement. 'I'd like to kiss you again,' she said at last. 'I'd like for you to kiss me, gently and respectfully, whatever it is you think I need, and we'll see how that goes. I might like it more than our earlier kisses. I might not. I'll let you know.'

She would like it more. She had to—for his sanity. He didn't know what he'd do if she liked it greedy and rough, because that wasn't him. He wasn't drawn to explore the darker sides of desire, those places where control bled away and chaos slipped in. Regardless of whether she was willing to accommodate him.

One kiss, and this time he'd do right by her, ease in slow with the barest touch of his lips against hers. Plenty of room for her sigh and his relief as her eyes fluttered closed as he slanted his head and fitted his lips more firmly against hers. Waiting rather than demanding her compliance, and there it was, the tip of her tongue skating along the edge of his upper lip, and he was careful, so careful to follow her cues and keep his hands to himself. Easy, never mind the want that pushed up from those places he always kept hidden. Sweet, because first kisses should be savoured, not driven into someone with the force of a fist.

He pulled back slowly, letting the space between their lips grow, watching her face come back into focus, pale and perfect, and her eyes open to regard him steadily.

'Better?' he asked and she smiled ever so slightly.

'Different.'

He could do better. Another kiss, this time with the reins less tightly held. Letting slip, just a little, to allow for a response that wasn't so carefully composed. She responded beautifully, so willing to follow where he led, so open to whatever he wanted to bestow. Enough to make a blush light her cheeks and her eyes look unfocused. Enough to risk his thumb against her lips when his mouth wasn't there, smoothing them, learning them, setting everything back in order because he couldn't have it any other way. 'Better?'

'Is this what you want from a wife? Someone who'll never truly know your heart because you're too busy hiding beneath all that delicious self-control?'

'Don't push me.' Even as he pressed her bottom lip lightly against her teeth. Not hurting her, no. And yet. 'Rule number one of the Arunian monarchs: don't ever lose control.'

'And what's rule number two?'

'An eye for an eye.'

He dropped to his knees in front of her and tugged the towel from her body. He pressed his lips to a bead of water that sat at the junction of her perfectly toned thighs. She gasped, and it was all the encouragement he needed. Hands sliding up her thighs to part them. The taste of her sweet on his tongue, and just like that he was ravenous again, licking and striking, flicking and sucking, listening and responding to every sound and twitch she gifted him with. He was good at this.

And she was so utterly, gloriously responsive. *Virgin.*

A virgin he should have left alone or, failing that, someone whose pleasure should have very definitely come before his own. His shaft twitched, only this time he ignored it. He'd taken his pleasure. Now it was her turn.

Her fingers came up to guide his head with more force than expected. But then, this slip of a woman knew exactly how to wield swords and knives and even sharper words.

A ragged curse that felt like an endearment. A trembling 'oh' when he redoubled his efforts.

He wanted her to say his name again as she came.

Words that seemed lost beneath her quiet gasps and his growls when he grew greedy and still couldn't get enough.

She came on his tongue, tense and trembling, and he could swear he felt the ripples of her body beneath his hand, and he should have withdrawn then, done and done, but there was always one more taste he had to have, even if he did avoid her most sensitive areas, and then she was dropping to her knees to face him and her hands were on his shoulders, and she said, 'Kiss me again and mean it, Augustus,' and his name on her lips was like a promise, so he did as she asked and knew himself for lost.

'Don't,' he whispered, when he finally found the will to pull away from her. 'Don't tempt me.'

This time, when he left, he made it all the way back to his quarters before shedding his clothes and stepping beneath a scalding shower in a futile effort to cleanse his soul.

Don't make me lose control.

Physical activity was the only thing that prevented Augustus from climbing the walls in the days that followed. He swam until he either had to get out of the pool or drown, he ran on the treadmill in his private gym until he bent double and emptied his stomach. He put his recently purchased catamaran through its paces until he found its tipping point and it still didn't take the edge off.

He tried burying himself in work, which worked until his put-upon secretary demanded an assistant.

He went on a date with a perfectly eligible woman who was charming and accomplished and didn't challenge his self-control one little bit. He hated every awkward, stilted moment of it.

He visited Theo's cousin Benedict to look at horseflesh and met the long-term mistress of Theo's father, who just so happened to own the horses they were looking at, and he'd stood in the stables and wanted to ask her what it was like to own the heart of a king but never to hold his hand in public. In the end he didn't ask because he didn't have the right to pry and he probably wouldn't have liked the answer anyway.

Benedict, after spending half a day with him, dropped all pretence of pleasantries the minute they left the stables and brought out the bolt-cutters in an attempt to prise Augustus open.

'What on earth is wrong with you?' he demanded bluntly. 'I've seen junkies desperate for their next fix in better shape than you.'

And Benedict would know. Even though he'd settled down and returned to the family fold after his father's death, there wasn't much Benedict of Liesendaach didn't know about the darker side of sex, drugs and reckless self-indulgence.

'I'm not on drugs.' He'd never followed that road.

'And yet you're radiating barely concealed angst all over my calm. Are you having an existential crisis? You'd be surprised how many people invite me to tea and then proceed to come undone. As if I give a damn.' Benedict was eyeing him speculatively. 'Although for you I might show minor concern. I owe your sister a favour. She gave me my cousin back.'

'Whatever debt you think you owe Moriana, leave me out of it.' He didn't need saving or fixing or whatever else Benedict thought he was doing. He just wanted a distraction from the woman in his birdcage who was messing with his head. The woman who this morning had put a tapestry illustrating one of his ancestors feasting in the round room on show in the main entry hall. The accompanying plaque named every nobleman in the picture, the names of every courtesan and the date. On a plinth beside the tapestry sat an open recipe book, written in a language of old. Beside it, she'd offered a printed translation of *Feast Number Six for Midwinter Dining*.

Augustus scowled afresh. Sera of the High Reaches was doing exactly what he'd told her to do and, what was more, she was doing it well.

'No sexual identity crisis?'

What the hell was it with these questions lately? 'I'm male. I'm straight. I sincerely don't know what else to say to that question.'

'Not a problem,' said Benedict blithely. 'But if that *had* been your problem I would have helped. I take my role seriously when it comes to being a guiding light for same sex relationships of the royal variety.'

'You buried yourself in vice, became estranged from your family and then downplayed your most important romantic relationship for years.'

'And now I'm back. Like I said: guiding light. I'm a veritable lighthouse.'

Augustus snorted.

'Besides, there are other existential crises to be had,' continued Benedict. 'No unexpected desire to be tied, gagged and at someone's mercy?'

'No.'

'Bootlicking, public sex, voyeurism…'

'I worry about you occasionally,' said Augustus.

'I'm worried for you right now, in spite of my self-proclaimed indifference. It appears I'm getting soft.'

'Worry about something else.'

'I hear you have a courtesan in residence. Moriana thinks it's wonderful. A revelation, rich in art, history and cultural significance. Which, while I embrace your sister's enthusiasm for all things cultural, rather seems to be missing the point. You have a woman who has been trained to indulge your every sexual whim living in your birdcage. How's that working out for you?'

Trust Benedict to get straight to the sexual point.

'The Lady Sera has now retired from her former role as courtesan and has taken on an events management and PR position.'

Benedict had his head down and his hands in his pockets as they headed for the car that would take them on to future engagements, but at this he looked up. 'No special services at all?'

'She's finding me a wife.'

When Benedict laughed, he did it body, heart and soul. He was laughing now, near bent double, and all Augustus could do was scowl.

'That's the worst idea you've ever had,' offered Benedict when his amusement no longer threatened his ability to talk.

'Thank you for your enduring support. Moriana's helping her.'

'Good heavens, you're serious.'

'When am I not?'

'Says he who threatened Theo with a procession of elephants after he proposed to your sister.'

'I reiterate—when am I not serious?' Elephants too had been part of Arun's lore of old. His courtesan could probably tell him all about them. 'I need a wife in order to make the courtesan in the birdcage go away. I also need an heir and Arun could use a Queen. They seem like good enough reasons to make marrying a priority.'

'I understand your need for a wife. I even understand your desire to canvass other royal opinions as part of your decision-making process. But why's the courtesan helping you choose one?'

'She's not helping me choose, she's simply helping to organise the parade of eligible women.'

'Giving her ample opportunity to manipulate the parade itself,' Benedict offered with a hefty helping of sarcasm.

'If I don't like what I see I can always look elsewhere.' Augustus was famously picky when it came to choosing women to keep company with. 'It's not as if I haven't already looked. I need to broaden my horizons. This is one way to do it.'

'Are you intending to bed your former courtesan while you wait for your potential Queen to amble by?'

'No.' But his brain conjured the image of Sera on her knees before him and then another one of her naked beneath him, a writhing, pleading mess as he sent her soaring, those expressive grey eyes blind to everything but the feel of him. 'That would be potentially off-putting to said future wife.'

'Tempting, though.'

'Very,' he admitted through gritted teeth.

Benedict smirked. 'I see your dilemma. Fewer scruples would help.'

'A king leads by example. Sera of the High Reaches needs to leave my employment in the same state in which she entered it.'

'Right. And meanwhile you…'

'Go slowly round the twist, yes.'

Sera knew Augustus was avoiding her and, frankly, that suited her just fine. Courtesans weren't meant to blush at the memory of a man's mouth on her. She wasn't supposed to crave Augustus's attention the way she did. Anything would do. A touch, a glance, the merest shred of his attention. Anything to feed the bubbling cauldron of emotion he'd awakened in her. The desperate need to satisfy his desires and hers. The things they could *do*, and *feel*. They could be fearless together…

She read texts on controlling sexual situations, because that was his way, was it not? She read texts on how best to stay safe while surrendering control. She did everything he asked of her. Put artwork from the High Reaches on display in his palace and the libraries and galleries of Arun. Arranged speaking engagements for herself and spent hours crafting speeches to fit various target audiences. She set about reinventing her role here and part of her relished the challenge even as another part mourned the loss of tradition. She purchased clothes more suitable to a corporate banker than a courtesan, and when the Winter Solstice ball came along she attended it as the events co-ordinator, dressed fully in nondescript black. Black boots, black trousers, fitted black blazer and her black hair pulled back in a high ponytail. Communication pack at her waist and an earphone in her ear, she was quite clearly working the event and not there as a guest.

It didn't stop people—mostly men—from staring at her regardless or luring her to their side under the guise of making a complaint and then asking for her phone number or simply asking her what she was doing later. No finesse, but most accepted her polite brush-offs with equal civility. Those who pressed their suit met Ari and Tun. Augustus might have requested her presence here tonight but he hadn't been stupid enough to leave her unprotected.

Small mercies.

Just because he had no desire for a courtesan, didn't mean others were equally restrained. Augustus had relinquished his claim on her in the most public way possible—by putting her to work, very visibly, in another role. Others were singularly inclined to pick her up where he'd left off.

It made it extremely difficult for her to competently do her job.

When Augustus's long-suffering secretary caught her eye and wordlessly directed her to the service doors, Sera made her way towards them. He met her there, his face impassive.

'The King respectfully requests that from

this point onwards you leave all requests for your personal attention for either me or your guards to deal with,' he began.

'With pleasure.'

'He also requests that you stop deliberately attracting attention.'

Deliberately attracting attention? 'Are my black clothes not modest enough?'

The older man hitched his shoulders in a wordless gesture signifying who knew what.

'Shall I overcome years of comportment training and walk with a slouch?'

Another shrug. 'I'm just the messenger.'

'Then you can tell the King that this is no more and no less attention than I ever receive. People look and people want. There is no "off" switch. The relationship between King and courtesan is often mutually beneficial in that once he stakes his claim the unwanted attention afforded a courtesan will *stop*. Of course, *this* King is far too enlightened to understand that the course of action he insists I follow has consequences he knows nothing about.'

'I'll let him know,' the older man said, and strode off.

The next time a guest beckoned her forward, she sent Ari to deal with him.

The next time the King's secretary approached she summoned her gentlest smile.

'The King suggests you supervise the event from the upper west balcony,' he said. 'From behind the lights.'

'Of course.' There were two ways to reach the suggested balcony. By the servants' entrance or by the central staircase. She chose the stairs. Head held high and the six-inch heels of her boots very much on show, she made her way straight up the middle with Tun and Ari falling into place on either side of her and two steps behind. She didn't bother looking back.

She knew damn well she had almost everyone's attention. Including Augustus's.

He found her two hours later, after the remains of the meal had been cleared away and guests had gravitated towards the dance floor, some to dance, some to stand and mingle at the edges. He'd mingled too, for as long as his patience would allow, and then he'd slipped away through a side door and taken the back way to the balcony. She had her back to him as one of her guards opened the door so he could enter. The second guard appraised him coolly before apparently making some kind of deci-

sion and silently taking his leave and closing
the balcony door behind them and plunging
them into near darkness.

'Why are you up here when you should be
down there?' she asked without even turning
around.

Why indeed? 'How did you know it was me?'

'Ari gave us privacy. There's only one person in this palace he'd do that for without waiting for my command.' She turned to face him.
'Your Majesty.'

He didn't make the mistake of thinking Sera's guards were under his control. According
to his Head of Security, they were compliant
to a point. Co-operating when they could, fit-
ting unobtrusively into whatever protection
detail was in place. Beyond that, they were
hers. 'Lucky me.'

Her shuttered glance mocked him.

'Would you prefer I call him back in?' she
offered, dry as dust.

'No. The evening didn't go quite to plan, as
far as you were concerned.'

'Didn't it?' She sounded wholly unconcerned. 'I thought it went well. You mingled.
Ate well. Met the women you wanted to meet.
I gather Katerina DeLitt is a pleasant enough
conversationalist.'

'She is.' One of his sister's additions to the potential brides list. A noblewoman with strong trade connections. 'She's titled, well-read, entertaining and perfectly pleasing to the eye. And yet no one here this evening seemed to be able to see past you.'

'It happens.'

'Why?' His knew his voice sounded tight with frustration. 'You were supposed to blend in as an employee, shatter the myth of the courtesans of old. Instead you—'

'Instead I what?' He really should have taken note of the sharp note in her voice. He hadn't grown up with a temperamental sister for nothing. 'Did I not dress appropriately and make sure the evening ran smoothly? Was I not available to troubleshoot guest issues as they arose? Did I not do what you asked of me?'

'You drew too much attention.'

She leaned back against the balcony and crossed her arms in front of her, wholly unconcerned by the low balustrade and the significant drop to the floor below. 'I've been drawing that kind of attention since childhood. They say I have too much presence, that my beauty serves to make others insecure. Some people want to tear me down before I've ever said a word to them. Others would own me for their own ego enhancement. I don't blend in. I never have. My beauty will always be both celebrated and demonised, sometimes both at once, because beauty is power, and never more dangerous than in the hands of someone who knows how to use it.' She cocked her head to one side, her face in shadows and the spotlights behind her shining out across the ballroom below. 'You want me to craft a new persona while I live beneath your roof and I have no objection to doing so. But the response of others to power such as mine is always going to be part of it. *Your* response to me is always going to be part of it. So what's it to be? Are you here to work with me? Ask me to set up another meeting for you with the pleasant enough Katerina DeLitt? Perhaps you'd also like to tell me to make a note to never invite Peter Saville and Ricardo Anguissey to the same event again lest their wives and everyone else discover that they're in each other's pants? Or are you here to condemn me because my mere presence makes others behave badly?'

He'd been about to do that last one. He hadn't liked the attention his guests had bestowed on his new events co-ordinator. The predatory nature of some of it. His instinctive desire to protect her from it. He'd wanted to claim her, to own her, to tear into anyone who dared covet her. Berate her for using the same stairs dozens of his other employees had used throughout the evening.

He wanted to step away from the door and look into her face, the better to try and interpret her every thought. He wanted to see her eyes darken with desire not hurt, and then he wanted to turn her around to face the ballroom and tell her that none of the people down there mattered; only his elemental desire to claim her mattered. And then he would step up behind her, open her trousers and bring her to quivering arousal with his fingers while his mouth ravaged hers and smothered her soft gasps of completion. She'd let him.

He knew damn well she'd let him.

And the next time he saw her she'd have drawn up a new list of candidates eligible to become his Queen—women with a knack for surrendering to exhibitionism or possessiveness or whatever this was that he wanted from her.

From *her*, not them.

'Is my Minister for Trade really having an affair with our Liesendaach Ambassador?' he said instead. 'I'll have to tell Theo.'

'You're assuming he doesn't already know.'

Augustus lowered his head and bit down a snort. She had a point. 'In that case, I'll ask my sister why I shouldn't simply send Liesendaach's diplomatic representative home and get them to send a new one.'

She smiled ever so slightly, and dropped her arms to her sides and then curled her hands around the railing behind her. 'That would be one way of opening dialogue about the conflict of many interests, yes.'

He liked seeing her less defensive when she looked at him. 'What else did you see?'

'Your Transport Minister's wife is pregnant and not coping well with the demands of his job and her first trimester sickness. One of the Cordova twins of Liesendaach will be going home this evening with your Horse Master, although I'm not sure which one. And Prince Benedict of Liesendaach enjoys winding you up more than you can possibly imagine. If he wasn't so enamoured of his partner I'd think him desperate for your attention.'

'Benedict enjoys cultivating other people's low opinion of him. It prevents them from noticing how ruthlessly cunning he is until it's too late. At which point he usually has enough dirt on them to make them beholden to him for life. Never underestimate him.'

'I like him already,' she murmured.

'He collects art. I'm sure he'd like to see some of the treasures that now reside in the round room.' Benedict would go nuts over the tapestry wheel on the floor. 'You might want to be careful about where he wants to sit on that round sofa of yours. Because he'll doubtless want to sit in every damn section, just to see what happens.'

She smiled and for a moment his breath caught in his throat. It didn't matter what they'd just been talking about because that smile was one he hadn't seen before—openly conspiratorial and at the same time unguarded. As if gossiping about guests and trusting her to deal with Benedict however she saw fit made her happy.

He looked away, trying desperately not to be one of those men who looked at her and wanted her for all the wrong reasons. Nor did he want to be among the masses who became putty in her hands with just one smile. He wanted to do right by this woman who'd been placed in his care regardless of whether he wanted her there or not. Set her up to succeed. Give her a way out of the lifestyle she'd had thrust upon her when she was seven years old.

No judgement. No slaking his desires. Just common human decency. 'Make sure Katerina DeLitt is invited to the next palace function, along with the next set of candidates,' he said gruffly. 'I like her.'

And then he left.

CHAPTER SIX

THREE DAYS LATER Sera stepped naked into the bathing pool and kept going until every part of her was underwater from the neck down. The pool had been getting warmer by the day and now it ran hot, day in and day out. No one used it but her. Augustus had declined, ever since that first time. Her guards declined the use of it—even if they knew she'd be out all day giving a talk at one gallery or another or being interviewed by journalists or overseeing this function or that. Augustus kept her busy and if he wasn't in residence, his secretary kept her busy. TV show hosts loved her because the cameras loved her face and she could string two words together.

She was compliant, carving out a place for herself in his world that had nothing to do with the sexual aspects of a courtesan's role and everything to do with social outreach and celebration of history and letting people get a behind-the-scenes glimpse of the day-to-day running of the palace.

She was an ambassador. Making connections, building a web, consolidating power that didn't belong to her, and the role suited her to perfection. She was good at it.

Augustus was managing her, piling on the work, keeping her so busy in her dual roles of palace PR and events management that there was barely time for thought, and far too little time for herself.

This morning she'd requested of his secretary that down time be built into her weekly schedule and that if she was obliged to work weekends she wanted the following Tuesday kept free for her own use.

'Finally,' she thought she'd heard the old man mutter beneath his breath, and then he'd pulled a file drawer open and moments later handed her a bunch of papers on workplace rights. 'Read these, sign these, hand them back in and I can most assuredly do something about that, Lady Sera. Not everyone here is willing to work like a dog for no apparent reason.'

She'd read through the employment conditions, signed them and handed them back in

and now had every full Tuesday, Wednesday
and Thursday morning off.

Much to Augustus's displeasure.

Sera ducked beneath the water, wetting her
hair and holding her breath until the need to
breathe forced her to rise.

Tomorrow was Tuesday, her first full day
off, and Ari had invited her to spar with him
during tomorrow's six a.m. lesson. She hadn't
sparred with anyone since Ari had dropped
her to the ground and Augustus had helped
her back up. She'd taken on a tutor's role instead, helping those who'd taken up the invitation to practise the forms, and she enjoyed
her role, but maybe tomorrow she *would* spar
with Ari again.

Take back some of her own identity.

If Augustus objected she would tell him she
was a tutor now and call it a demonstration.

As for the charities she'd been working for
so tirelessly, maybe it was time to invest some
of her own identity into that too.

And see what good and noble King Augustus would do.

'What do you mean she wants to take a courtesan's clothing collection on the road, starting with viewings at city brothels?'

Augustus knew he was glaring at his personal secretary but the idea was preposterous. He was doing everything in his power to *remove* her courtesan status. He was trying, above all, to render her role here respectable. The very *least* she could do was appreciate it.

'Lady Sera's guards put forward the security arrangement plans this morning,' his secretary informed him placidly. 'There's a fifty-page report justifying the social benefits involved, including collaboration with community welfare groups and backing from your police commissioner and city mayor. Two of the brothels are extremely prestigious. Others are less so. I have it on good advice that several are for…acquired tastes. They're all registered and legal.'

Silence was one response to situations out of his control. It wasn't the only response available to him. 'Get her in here. Now.'

'Lady Sera's schedule for the day puts her at the state library attending a history lecture until one. This afternoon she'll be overseeing the botanists' picnic on the lawn surrounding the royal glasshouses.'

Roses. Good grief. Roses and social welfare. Just what he needed.

'Ask the Lady Sera if she's available for dinner this evening. Put us in the blue dining room with several dishes for sharing, a small selection of sweets and let us serve ourselves.' It wasn't an unusual request, although it was one he usually reserved for family.

'Does next week's costume tour have your approval?' His secretary reminded him of the matter in hand.

'No. Have you read the proposal?'

'It makes for interesting reading. I particularly enjoyed Chapter Two.'

'Fifty pages, you say?'

'With references, footnotes and a reading list,' the older man said, handing it over. 'She's also written you a report outlining new initiatives for education reform, particularly with regard to non-academic children. She confirms a substantial donation from the temples of the High Reaches to set up a pilot project. You want to see that proposal too?'

'Give it over.' He didn't have time for this. He truly didn't.

'Additionally, Lady Sera has been restructuring the fund-raising portfolio related to education. The one your grandmother, mother and Moriana have toiled over for generations.'

'What for? What part of "It's a good one" doesn't she understand?'

'I'll leave that for you to judge. I'll warn you

though, she's already engaged your sister's co-operation and they're looking at some quite sweeping reforms.'

'They'll still have to go through me.' He wasn't looking forward to being the voice of reason. He could already name a dozen education initiatives that Moriana had wanted to support that had been shut down by various committees full of education experts. 'Let's dig deeper into Sera's background and education qualifications. Personal history too. I want no surprises when it comes to what kind of reforms she's likely to advance.'

'You have a dossier on her.'

'I have a CV. I want to expedite that full investigative report I ordered. Whatever has been collected, get them to send it.'

The older man nodded.

'As for education reform—'

'It's been on your agenda for the last six months,' the older man offered drily. 'You keep shuffling it to the bottom of your pile while you concentrate on regional water plans. I gave the portfolio to Lady Sera a week ago on a whim. So if you want to blame somebody for that particular report, blame me.'

'I will.' Augustus looked at the folder in his hand and scowled.

'Children are our future,' the older man said serenely. 'I so look forward to yours.'

'Alas, that will require a wife.' And, at last glance, he still didn't have one in mind.

He already gave careful consideration to the charities and initiatives he supported.

'Will you be requiring casual dress for dinner this evening or something more formal?' his secretary asked.

'Casual.' Even if the image of Sera in a formal evening gown made him momentarily lose focus. What would a courtesan of the High Reaches regard as formal clothing? What would she regard as casual? He hadn't forgotten the collar and the manacles she'd worn upon her arrival. 'Definitely casual.'

Sera arrived at the door to the blue dining room at precisely thirty seconds past seven. The door was open and Augustus was already within. She entered and he looked up, a dark-haired devil with classically handsome features and black eyes that knew how to drill deep.

She pushed back the hood of her travelling cloak and met those eyes with polite composure, before dropping to a curtsey and rising again before he could tell her to get up. He could add *Doesn't take orders* to her list of sins. There were bigger sins.

'You wear a travelling cloak to walk down a corridor?' Augustus asked as she reached for the tie at her neck and stepped aside so that Ari could wheel a covered rack of clothes into the room and set it to one side. She waited until Ari had stationed himself outside the door before closing it behind him and turning to face her host.

'You ordered me never to appear in front of your court wearing the clothing of my profession,' she reminded him gently. 'Remember?'

The cloak came off. Her tunic was sheer and the bodice beneath it was more beautiful and intricate than he had ever seen before. Fitted trousers, high heels, no jewellery but for the pearls in her hair. Modesty for the most part, enticement if anyone was so inclined. She draped the cloak over the back of a nearby chair and turned to face him again.

'You call that casual dress?' he asked.

'Yes. Also, you're wearing a hand-tailored suit, a fifty-thousand-dollar vintage watch, and the only concession you've made to dressing casually is that the top button of your shirt's undone and you've loosened your tie.' She arched an elegant eyebrow. 'Did you expect me to wear shorts?'

'I'm pretty sure the watch wasn't worth fifty thousand when my grandfather bought it,' he offered mildly. 'But point taken. You look lovely.' She always did, no matter what she wore.

He ought to be used to it by now.

'I know your interest in historical gowns and clothing is limited,' she said, turning towards the clothes rack. 'But I took the liberty of bringing a few along for show and tell. They'll form part of the costume collection I'd like to take on the road to various places, should you give the go-ahead.'

Which sounded all well and good, but he'd read the proposal—all fifty pages of it and the appendices—and by *various places* she meant brothels.

Augustus would have reprimanded her for being so blatantly obvious about her political agenda, only she'd turned her back on him and his attention had been firmly caught and held by the dazzling dragon-shaped embroidery that wove through the material at her back, leaving pockets of nothing but creamy skin showing through the delicate gaps. Shimmery scales collected from heaven only knew what kind of beast highlighted various dips and curves, and as for those forest-green stilettoes that matched one of the dragon's main colours, how did she even balance on those things?

'Would you like a drink?' he asked, rather than engage with the topic she'd introduced. He was no novice when it came to directing conversation where he wanted it. Or keeping people off-balance, if he wanted to.

Movement was good. Movement meant he could leave the dragon at her back behind. The sideboard was stacked with a selection of beverages. 'Wine?'

'Thank you.' Sera smiled, her movements quick and effortless as she removed one particular gown from the rack and twirled it around on its hanger, the better to make the skirt flare. 'Take this gown, for example.'

'No. Sera, you're not taking it anywhere.'

Her eyes turned stormy. 'You haven't heard me out.'

'Red or white?'

'White.'

He poured some into a wine glass and took it to her and their fingers touched.

Her gaze met his and the outside world as he knew it skidded to a halt as a kaleidoscope of memories flashed through his brain. Sera on her knees in front of him, swallowing him down. Sera rising naked from the bathing pool and wringing water from her hair. Sera pushing back the hood of her travelling cloak. Sera, all too tempting, no matter what she said or did.

Perfect posture, regal bearing. He wondered if it came naturally to her or whether it had been drummed into her by her elders, the way Moriana's had been ground into her. The way cool analysis and never letting anyone get close enough to truly know him had been drummed into him.

'Is there a reason you don't trust me to do a good job with this?' she asked. 'Have I not been pitch-perfect in my presentation of the courtesans of old so far?'

'You have.' He had to give her that. 'Different audience.'

'You mean you'd rather not put me in front of an audience that might actually *benefit* from their profession being acknowledged and treated with respect?'

'You can reach them without prioritising them. You already are.'

'But I want to prioritise them.'

'Why?'

'You've never lived at the edge of poverty

and violence and hopelessness, have you?' She waved a careless hand in his direction. 'No need to answer; I know you haven't. But I have. And every day I thank my looks and my luck and the training someone saw fit to grace me with that I'm not still there.'

'I can't imagine you there.' He just couldn't.

'My mother was once a courtesan to a high-born man. She loved him, and in many ways that precipitated her downfall because I don't believe he ever loved her at all. He just wanted her at his beck and call. He certainly didn't want me to ever draw breath. My mother fled, but his reach was long. She tried to start over, but he always found her. She hid, and once I was born she hid us both, over and over again, always moving, always one step ahead. The houses got smaller. The cupboards got barer. Her sponsors meaner.'

He didn't like this history she was telling him, but he listened while she paced.

'I don't remember all that much of the very early years but, by the time I was seven, my mother was lost in the bottle and dying of can-cer and I was so skinny and malnourished that I couldn't even sit at a table and eat the first meal Lianthe ever put in front of me. I ate a quarter of it, and even that was too much for me. To this day I still prefer to snack rather than sit down to a three-course meal.' She spared a glance for the dinner table. 'I trust it's simply an eating preference by now but it was born of necessity.'

'Why are you telling me this?' About the food. Her mother and the bottle.

'You ask me why I proposed the costume tour of the brothels and this is part of it. It's personal for me. This lavish, glittering history of the Kings' courtesans is their history too, and you have no idea what simple acknowledgement can mean to those who are outcast. Those who live on the fringes of society and who are so often overlooked. I'm already reaching out and talking to your noble art curators and librarians about the history of courtesans—at your request. Why *not* reach out to the people who identify with that history the most?'

She was warming to her theme and he couldn't take his eyes off the glittering, shimmering dragon which writhed on her back.

'Education and learning. Physical and mental health. Those are causes the Arunian royal family has supported for centuries.' Irony tinged her voice. 'Causes you continue to endorse and pour money and resources into. My costume tour proposal should have made sense to you. I designed it to fit within your broader mission statements.'

Too smart by half. Too bold with her plans. And defiantly, unapologetically idealistic. He wondered if he'd ever been like that when it came to what causes to support. He rather thought not. 'It fits to a point,' he said carefully. 'I applaud your…passion for outreach.'

'No, you don't. You'd rather bury it. Turn me into a perfect puppet who performs whatever tasks you deem suitable for someone like me.'

'What I'd rather do is protect you,' he argued. 'Keep the press off your back and your reputation spotless by only giving you certain roles to play. If I send you to brothels the press will draw comparisons to what you do here, for me. They'll dig up your history, make front page news out of you.'

'So? I'm not ashamed of my pathway through life. I am who I am. You think you're protecting me—you're not. You think that by carving away at the unsavoury parts of me you're reshaping me into something better. You're not. All you're doing is carving me up.'

Sera's hands trembled as she cupped her wine glass and brought it to her lips. She made a good show of wetting those lips but he'd bet his kingdom on the fact that she didn't swallow so much as a drop. He strode to the sideboard, poured her a glass of water and exchanged it for the wine before she could protest.

'Why say yes to wine when you don't even drink?' he snapped.

She took the water and drank it down, not stopping until she'd finished, and then set the glass on the table. 'Is that a no to taking the costumes on tour throughout your city brothels?'

'Yes, it's a no. You're not doing it. It's a bad idea.'

She looked strangely shattered as she collected her cloak and fastened it around her neck. 'As always, I am bound to your will and will abide by your command. Now, if you'll excuse me, I'll take my leave.'

'Sera.' Her compliance should have pleased him. Instead, it left him strangely bereft. 'You could stay and eat.'

Not that she ate in the same way he did, apparently. She'd already told him that.

'And talk about what?' she asked coolly. 'Adding perfection to the list of things you require in a wife? No supporting those lost causes, right? No acknowledging the seething, need-ridden underbelly of humanity from that pedestal she'll be standing on, right? Consider it done.'

'I didn't say that.' She could get under his skin faster than any woman he'd ever known. Call up a temper he took a great deal of care to conceal. He still had her glass of wine in his hand. The temptation to drink it was strong. His fingers tightened on the stem. That tiny insignificant tell did not go unnoticed by his courtesan.

'Go on.' She drew closer and closer still until her breath fanned his ear and the scent of tea roses teased his nose. 'Throw it.'

'Why would I do that?' He set the glass on the table gently, never mind that the temptation to hurl it at the nearest wall was strong. 'I'm not a savage.'

'I guess they carved that out of you as a child.' She drew closer and closer still until her lips touched his ear. He shuddered and not with disgust. She didn't miss that tell either. 'Who needs passion? Who needs compassion? Not a king.'

'There's nothing wrong with cool calculation,' he argued. It was what he'd been raised to believe. 'Passion's overrated.'

'If you truly believe that, I pity you.' Her hand snaked up to fist in his hair and he made no move to stop her. 'You should have just thrown the glass.'

'The world might have ended if I had.'

'It wouldn't have.'

The kiss, when she dragged his head down and lifted her lips to his, was searingly hot and decidedly angry. It brought him to full and throbbing hardness in the space of thirty seconds. If this was punishment for his refusal to accommodate her wishes, he'd take it. If it was a thirst she couldn't control, he'd slake it. If this was her way of trying to make him change his mind, good luck with that.

She drew back all too soon as far as he was concerned, but he wasn't the one running this little power play; she was. He'd figure out what that kiss meant soon enough.

'You're a good king, Augustus. No one can deny it.' She let go of his hair, took a breath, stepped back. 'I hope one day you get to be human too.'

He waited until she and her dragon and her rack full of courtesans' clothing had left the room. He shut the door behind her and counted to ten, and then ten again, before striding across to the table and draining her wine glass.

He let anger, frustration for all the things he could not do, and aching desire for all the things he could not have fill him. He flung the wine glass at the fireplace, where it smashed into glittering pieces.

And the world did not end.

The following day didn't begin well for Augustus of Arun. He'd slept poorly and risen with the sun. He'd gone to the kitchen to find his own breakfast, only to overhear two of his catering staff talking about how Sera's guards had put on a fighting display with long sticks yesterday morning, apparently, and the hits had come thick and fast and left everyone who watched in awe. They fought in the covered stable area these days, not because he'd given his tacit approval but because of the sawdust on the ground and the space and relative privacy it afforded them. Augustus wondered if they fought there because any gathered crowd could melt away into the shadows fast if they were discovered.

He grabbed a bread roll straight from the oven, ripped it open and cut the end from a length of resting roast beef, and knew for a fact that he wouldn't have got away with either action had he still been a child.

He cut through the back door and headed for the stables. He found the crowd easily enough and it looked like a regular martial arts lesson to him, with Ari leading and Tun and Sera helping the trainees with the movements. Sera still practised the forms with her guards on a daily basis, so he'd been informed, but she hadn't sparred since that day he'd hauled her off the ground.

Two men standing in front of him sent him startled looks and shuffled to the side but he shook his head and gestured for them to stay where they were. He didn't want to be noticed this morning. He just wanted to watch.

When Ari told the class they would be doing the form one last time from start to finish, Sera and Tun fell into step with him, making it look effortless. And when that was done and everyone had bowed and the class had been dismissed, Ari and Sera moved over to a canvas holdall and unzipped it and rolled it out along the ground—it was like no holdall he'd ever seen. More like a portable armoury.

Ari selected two wickedly curved short swords with black handle grips, while Sera selected similar, only her grips were red. They sat in her hands as if they'd been made for her. Maybe they had. The form they practised next had its origins in the one they'd practised in class, that much he could see, the lines of their bodies extended by glittering curved knives.

They made it look as if they'd been born holding knives and cutting patterns in the air.

And then Sera said something to Ari and he frowned, and she smiled back at him sharp and sure and broke from her pattern and moved to face him, not quite head-on, a little to one side. They bowed to each other, plenty of space between them. Tun came to stand between them as a referee would in a boxing ring. At his word he stepped back and they began to fight.

If anyone thought they'd hold back because of the lethal weapons in their hands, they thought wrong.

The fighting was fast and vicious, with Sera on the attack and Ari defending, and Augustus felt his breath lodge somewhere in his throat. Ari was bigger, stronger and his reach was longer and still Sera came at him, even when he began to strike back. The clash of swords rang in his ears, broken only by the occasional murmur from those watching.

He thought about stopping the fight. Demonstration. Whatever it was, he thought about stopping it, but there was no way he wanted to break their concentration. Absolute focus and unearthly skill was all that stood between them and a potentially fatal blow.

And then, between one moment and the

next, Ari was on his back on the ground and Sera was on top of him, the curve of one blade at his neck and the other poised to take his upraised hand off at the wrist.

The man in front of Augustus swore silently beneath his breath, and Augustus knew that by lunchtime the palace would be buzzing with the news that the courtesan of the High Reaches was some kind of mystical warrior in addition to being the Devil's temptress.

Surely she'd been sitting on the fallen sword master for far too long.

He watched her roll off and to her feet as if she'd heard him. Tun clapped once and she and Ari moved close for quick smiles and quiet conversation as they released their fighting grips on the blades and began to examine the edges of them. All in a day's work. Nothing unusual about what they'd just demonstrated.

Who were these people?

She saw him out of the corner of her eye and started to walk towards him. People melted away as if sensing conflict. All except for her guards, who stayed right where they were, neither courting conflict nor avoiding it.

'Is that your way of blowing off steam?' he asked.

'It works.'

He'd been thinking about her words from last night. Her scorn for his cool calculation and his need to control what he could. 'You want to know what I see when you're out there passionately blowing off steam?' He didn't wait for an answer. 'Absolute control.' His gaze skipped towards Ari. 'And lives utterly dedicated to the quest for it.'

'Why are you here?' she asked next.

'I've been thinking about what you said last night and all the things I didn't say. The personal things that might have helped you understand my reluctance to have you reach out to a bunch of brothels.'

She waited for him to speak, and he didn't want to, he really didn't, but she'd shown him her heart last night and her passion and maybe they would understand each other a little better if she knew his.

'When I was fifteen I had my first kiss. She was a stable girl, several years older than me, and she'd been lobbying for that kiss for at least three years. It was pretty chaste, as far as kisses went, but she sold her story to the papers that afternoon and we all read about it at breakfast the following morning.'

The lecture his father had given him still had the power to make him wince.

'The woman I finally lost my virginity to was an older woman as well—a woman with enough money and power and sheer front to withstand the hounding of the press for months. Just long enough for me to feel safe in her arms. And then she turned around and finally granted that press interview and laid me bare.

'She called me an accomplished lover—and I was by then—and then added that I could also be a little too passionately intense for some tastes. She told them she envied me my brilliant mind and in the same breath warned of sweeping social and economic reforms once I took the throne. I'd made the mistake of talking to her about the causes I was passionate about, you see. I'd talked big bold plans that didn't have a hope of seeing the light of day— not then. Not without years of careful planning. The press called me an ignorant, idealistic fool and I was—I was a fool to think I could confide in her or trust her. She praised my protective nature, especially when it came to those I consider family, and then casually mentioned how rigidly impenetrable I could be when it came to letting other people in.'

None of it true. All of it true.

'Which was quite the complaint because, as

far as I was concerned, I *had* let her in. Like a fool.'

Sera opened her mouth to speak but he put his hand up to stop her.

'And now you, a courtesan sent here specifically to serve me, wants to go into the brothels and talk job descriptions, and they're going to have questions art curators and librarians would never dare ask you. Questions about me and what I want and need and think and who's to say you won't expose me?'

'I would never do that.' She drew herself up and still didn't manage to reach his shoulder. Bare feet. A face flushed with exercise. 'I am a courtesan of the High Reaches. Confidentiality is the key to our *existence*, and beyond that...' She shook her head. 'Augustus, I will never betray your confidences. Not sexual, emotional or intellectual. You have my word. My oath. That's what you *get* when you get me. A safe space in which to simply be human.'

'I want to believe you.' He looked away from those earnest grey eyes. Experience suggested he shouldn't.

'I can't make that decision for you,' she offered quietly.

He nodded. He'd think on it. 'There was another reason I came out here this morning,' he said, while in the distance a stablehand worked on a horse's hoof with a file.

'What is it?'

He couldn't even bring himself to look at her while he was saying it. 'I love the way you move.' It was as simple and as complicated as that. 'I envy the fierce blend of passion and control you bring to everything you do and it's never more evident than when you're out there, facing an opponent. It's beautiful.'

It was the first thought he'd shared in years without analysing the pros and cons of doing so.

And it was met with complete and utter silence.

He glanced back, just in time to see a softly startled smile cross her face.

'I…thank you,' she said.

And the world did not end.

'What do you want done with the costume tour proposal?' Augustus's secretary asked him two hours later.

Augustus ran a hand across his face and memories flashed before him. Sera with a blade in each hand and total concentration on her face. Sera with a dragon on her back and her face alight with pleasure. Sera, who never failed to stand out, no matter what kind of company she was in, and who had yet to set a foot wrong in public.

Sera as a child, with a plate full of food in front of her that she could not eat. A plate that was only there in the first place because someone had *seen* her plight rather than turn away from an outcast child struggling for existence.

Sera's proposal to reach out to her sisters in service had healthcare and educational elements, but first and foremost it was about acknowledging their existence.

She could have been one of them. *Was* one of them, for all her finery and expensive education, and he'd never met a woman more accomplished.

Her mother had been one of them. A broken one.

This was no soulless, rudderless outreach programme. Sera had this one covered. He could trust her not to make this all about him. Couldn't he?

He dropped his hand and searched his heart and not his head.

'Green-light it,' he said.

CHAPTER SEVEN

THE INAUGURAL COURTESAN costumes tour, starting at a seedy but legal downtown brothel and finishing at the National Art gallery of Arun, received some of the best press Augustus had ever seen. It brought together six health and education outreach programmes already in place and cemented Arun's reputation as a progressive nation with the welfare and education of *all* its people at heart. Far from damaging his personal reputation, he was being hailed as a saviour. A man that any woman, courtesan or not, would be proud to have in their corner. He'd even accompanied Sera on one of the tours, to watch her in action and lend his support, and there'd been not one single, solitary crack about him partaking of her sexual services.

It was a God-given miracle.

Suffice to say, the fund-raising dinner he was currently attending suffered a little in comparison, even if Sera had organised it. The dinner helped raise funds for cancer research and had been on his social calendar for the past seven years running. He was seated next to Katerina DeLitt at his request and the lady was well aware of it. To her credit, she was socially adept and inclusive of the others around them. She had a charming smile and the kind of effortless poise he was used to. She had yet to hold his attention for long but maybe that was his fault for having Sera oversee the event.

Sera, with her tailored black suit and sky-high stilettos. Sera, with her hair coiled tightly into a bun at the nape of her neck and a face practically devoid of make-up. She didn't need make-up. She was quite beautiful enough.

He'd corner her afterwards for a crowd report and she'd tell him whom was currently at war with whom and other minor matters of interest. Her powers of observation kept his sharp too. Being able to one-up her in the observation stakes was wholly satisfying. Not to mention hard to do.

'She's very beautiful,' said Katerina DeLitt from somewhere beside him.

'Excuse me?'

Could be his attention had been somewhere

it shouldn't be, but he trusted Katerina DeLitt's manners to prevail and doubted she would repeat such a confronting statement.

'Lady Sera Boreas. She's very beautiful.'

'Ah.' Guess he was wrong. He eyed the woman seated to his left with renewed interest. She smiled wryly, diamond earrings dangling as she tilted her head the better to observe him.

'And talented too, assuming even half the things I hear about her are true,' she said next.

He knew full well he should steer the conversation elsewhere. Hard to court one woman when seemingly fixated on another. He could talk about the weather. The charity. Or horses—he had a fleeting memory of Katerina talking animatedly about horses.

Or he could succumb to curiosity. 'What kind of things do you hear?'

Katerina shrugged. 'She has great skill with knives, she can dance like a dream. She has a mind trained towards observation and is bound to you in ways no one can quite explain. You were forced by ancient laws to open your home to her. You can't get rid of her until you find a future wife and take steps to secure the throne. Even then, you might not let her go.'

'Sounds about right.' Katerina's information was good. 'Although I will let her go.'

'They say she has your ear, among other things. That she is your muse.'

Augustus frowned.

'Your Majesty, if I may be bold—and that does seem to be the best way to deal with you—what is it you want from me, when your attention is so obviously elsewhere?'

He appreciated her bluntness and returned it in full. 'I need a wife who will give me children and occupy the role of Queen Consort with all due diligence. Your name came up and I enjoy your company. I'm getting to know you.'

'I see. And what of love?' Katerina asked drily.

'Love can grow.'

'Your Ma—'

'Call me Augustus,' he interrupted.

'Augustus.' She said it nicely but not the way Sera did. 'Your Majesty, I know it's not fashionable, but let us be even more frank. As honoured as I am to have your attention, I'm in no hurry to put my heart on the line for you, knowing what else is available to you at any given time.'

'Meaning?'

She inclined her head towards Sera.

'That is not an option,' he grated. 'Sera will

leave once the terms of the accord have been satisfied. She may well leave before that if I can find a workaround.'

'But will your chosen Queen Consort ever be able to take her place? I have my doubts. Ask yourself this, my King in need of a Queen. When you walked in here this evening, who was the first person you looked for? Who did you *keep* looking for until she appeared?' Katerina smiled again, and it was a gentle smile, without malice. 'Be honest. Because it surely wasn't me.'

Another event, another debrief afterwards. That was the routine Sera and Augustus fell into over the weeks that followed. Sometimes they talked in his office and sometimes they used a small parlour in the west wing that he favoured, and sometimes, if he'd been held up after the event, he came to her quarters and sat within her sofa circle, always requesting a strategy session. Sera didn't mind it. She took quiet satisfaction in her ability to be of use to him, and if he kept his hands and his kisses carefully to himself while in her presence, so be it.

She didn't want to think about her growing need for his attention. The way her body craved his touch and her mind constantly circled back to him and what he was doing, how he was feeling. Whether he'd ever touch her again with the sole purpose of giving and taking pleasure.

She didn't want to admit she might be falling for him.

Nothing good had ever come of a courtesan falling for a king.

Tonight, Augustus's behaviour was different in that he stood staring at the request wheel at his feet for a good long while before turning to look at her. She'd been expecting him—maybe—and had changed out of her workwear into casual trousers and her customary tunic top. Nothing too sheer or revealing. No jewellery or make-up embellishment. The only concession she'd made to vanity was to let her hair down after she'd showered and not put it back up before opening her door to him. She liked the way he looked at it. The way he jammed his hands in his pockets as if to stop himself from reaching out to touch it.

The sexual attraction between them hadn't gone away, for all their business-based interactions. It simmered between them, thick and syrupy. Every glance, every pause, a study in denial.

For both of them.

'You know what I really want tonight?' he asked, and her brain helpfully supplied the perfect answer.

Me! You want me! Please take me!

'A toasted cheese sandwich.'

Or—or she could feed him. He wasn't even looking at her. 'That can be arranged,' she offered hospitably. 'Anything else?'

Me! Pick me!

'I wouldn't mind if it came with a glass of wine and some background music that I don't have to listen to as if it's the finest thing I've ever heard.'

'You didn't like the music gala this evening?'

'I liked it well enough but I was tired. Maintaining the fiction that I wanted to be there took more effort than usual.'

An honest response that painted him in a less than perfect light. A rare occurrence for this man who'd been trained from childhood to never show weakness or reveal any thoughts that could be used against him.

'Sit. Please.' She had music, food, and an excellent cellar full of wine on hand. 'I can feed you.' Cross off another scene on the pleasure wheel as done. It wasn't the sex scene she craved, granted, but it was progress.

'We can call for food,' he said.

'No!' Just…no. 'Does it matter who prepares it? I have a fully stocked kitchen. Why not let me put supper together?'

'You don't have to. That's not your role.'

'Always so hung up on roles.' He had no idea how much it pleased her when she was able to put her training to use and serve him. It wasn't a hardship. It was her pleasure. 'Many people take great pride and pleasure in being able to put food on the table and invite others to share it. It happens I'm one of them. Sit. Please.'

Please.

Sera didn't wait to see if he did her bidding, but when she returned he was sitting on the sofa in a different place to usual and the picture at his feet was that of people sharing a meal.

The wine she returned with was the best in the cellar and she knelt at his feet to pour it, faltering only when she went to hand it to him and found him watching her with hooded eyes that burned with a hunger that had nothing to do with food.

But he took it from her with a quiet, 'Thank you,' and if his fingertips touched hers, well, he'd said he was tired and it wasn't exactly light in here tonight with the moon behind a sky full of clouds. It wasn't warm in here either, beneath the glass dome, but he didn't seem to notice. Sera wanted to pretend that the tremble in her fingers as she released the wine was because of the cold, but self-deception had never been her friend. She'd shivered at the merest touch of his hand.

He said nothing more as she rose and turned some music on, soft and soothing.

He had his eyes closed and his head resting against the back of the sofa when she returned with the food. She'd brought extra: a small plate of honeyed pastries and a bowl of nuts. Sliced melon. Not a lot. Not a feast to make a person groan at the thought of eating it all.

'I hope some of that's for you too,' he murmured.

'It is.'

'Don't kneel at my feet, Sera. It might be what the picture shows and your courtesan training demands but I couldn't stand it.'

More weakness from him tonight, and he was deliberately letting her see it. She didn't know what to do with it. How to process it. So she sat and helped herself to some melon and then a glass of wine and sipped.

'You don't drink.' He was watching her, eyes still half closed.

'It's not that I don't drink at all. Sometimes when the vintage is very fine, I do.' She lifted her glass to the light and hid behind the poise the Order had instilled in her. Her relationship with alcohol was complicated. There was the way her mother had abused it. The way it lowered inhibitions and let devils in, false confidence in. But there were other things about it that deserved consideration. 'I learned about wine as part of my training. If you were to ask me to rank different areas of study, I'd put my study of wines and winemaking somewhere near the top, mainly because it's proven surprisingly useful. Everything from making small-talk with the high-flying wine aficionados of the world to tweaking wine selections for different charity functions so that the chefs are happy, the drinkers are happy and the hosts are not paying a fortune for it.'

He smiled and she wished he wouldn't, because it made her glow on the inside. Such a whore for his attention.

'And is there a wine to go with toasted cheese sandwiches?'

'There is, and we're drinking it.'

His smile widened. The glow inside her ignited and morphed into an open fire surrounded by a hearth.

In a family room.

'How are the owls?' he asked as he reached for a sandwich.

'They have names now,' she told him, taking on the mantle of conversation while he ate. 'Tomas and Claudia had lunch with me on Wednesday and we chose names then. I did notify your secretary Claudia was coming, and Tomas with her. I always ask permission to have visitors and provide details.' No exceptions.

Augustus shrugged, seemingly unconcerned. 'Some details stop at my secretary, especially if they're of no concern. How is Claudia?'

'She misses the freedom she had in the mountains.'

'Is that why she spends so much time with the falconer?'

'There could be another reason for that.' Augustus raised an eyebrow and this time it was Sera's turn to shrug. Far be it for her to lay Claudia's heart bare, although she had a fair idea where it lay. 'So, the smaller of the two owls is the male. His name is Orion. His larger companion is Ara, his mate, and he indulges her shamelessly. Their enemies are other owls of the same species and the occasional falcon. They're very adaptable and tend not to make their own nests, preferring instead to use nests abandoned by others, or make do with a man-made structure. Orion will fly down and perch on the trapeze on occasion, the better to see what I'm up to. He then reports back to Ara, who likes to pretend my activities are beneath her notice.'

'But they're not?'

'I've seen her watching me. She's more interested than she lets on.'

He'd finished the sandwich and was washing it down with wine. He looked more closely at the label on the bottle and then back at her.

'From the cellars of the Order of the Kite,' she said in answer to his question. 'They have quite the collection.'

'So I see. I know so little about this Order of yours. I have historians researching it, of course, but there are no experts to be found. Not amongst anyone I can get hold of.'

'What would you like to know?'

He snorted softly. 'Start at the beginning.'

'Of the history of the Order? It's over two thousand years old and began as a way for women in positions of power, or women close to men in positions of power, to connect and share journeys. They created a mountain retreat, a place of learning. Alliances were forged.

Daughters were positioned for particular roles within the world order of the day. Was a particular ruling court strong in trade but weak when it came to the comforts of its people? Who, from the pool of women available, was best placed to effect change? Occasionally, a ruler would reach out and request someone with particular connections and skills. If the Order could accommodate them, and it was perceived as being in their best interest to do so, they would.'

'Did the women of the Order ever have individual agendas or did they serve a higher cause?'

'I'm sure many have had their own agendas over the years. Politics is everywhere, and the Order is not immune. But on the whole I'd say the quest for balance, peace and prosperity guides all our members. I think of us as a benevolent force rather than a disruptive one.'

'I hate to break it to you, Sera, but taking up residence here in my palace and worming your way into my life and my thoughts…it's disruptive.'

'Am I not helping?' Pain lanced through her chest and she clamped her lips shut on a barrage of protest.

'In some ways you are. In other ways you're not helping at all.'

She didn't know what to say to that, and he didn't seem inclined to elaborate. Instead, he leaned back with his head against the back of the sofa and stared at the stars as if they had failed him.

'I was fourteen when I finally found this room,' he offered quietly. 'I'd been looking for it for years. I could see the dome from the sky, but the passageway to get here was boarded up and the room was out of bounds. Forgotten, until Moriana and I found it again and made it our own.' He pointed with his wine glass towards the platform halfway up the wall. 'We used to sit up there and shoot arrows into pumpkins down below. We damaged so many arrows when they struck stone instead of the target. I don't think we had a straight arrow left between us by the end of it all. I know we damaged the walls and the floors but I didn't care. Told myself I was striking back at the source of my discontent. The palace. The Crown. The expectations that rode me like a second skin. *Be worthy. Don't fail. Perform.* I was the Crown Prince—I had to perform. Everywhere except for here. There was no judgement here. I could curse and roar and take risks I could never take elsewhere. When I was in here, I could fly.'

Suspicion bloomed swiftly. 'You used the trapeze?'

'It's just a swing,' he offered mildly.

No safety net, half-rotted rope. No training. Dear God. 'And the adrenaline rush the first time you used it?'

'Pretty big.' He snorted softly. 'I thought this room would no longer feel like sanctuary once you claimed it. Figured if I stayed away my problem with you would go away, only I keep turning up at your door and you keep welcoming me in, offering me anything. You've no idea how much I want to claim you, and to hell with self-restraint and leading by example and kings not having courtesans in this day and age.'

'You could.' Her hands shook with the force of her need as she set her wine on the small side table. 'You could do that.'

'I'd make it so good for you.' He had a voice tailored for sin and seduction and lips that beckoned, even when his words were cruel. 'Treat you like a queen.'

'I don't want to be a queen,' she said, but he was drawing closer and she wasn't moving away.

'We all do things we don't particularly want to do.' He brushed his lips against hers and she opened for him instinctively, her tongue coming out to meet his. He slid a gentle hand beneath her hair and cupped the back of her neck, his thumb brushing the skin just behind her ear as he tilted her head where he wanted it and claimed her lips once more. Her eyes fluttered closed.

It was a kiss to get lost in.

When they broke it several years later, he rested his forehead against hers and drew a ragged breath. He ran his hand across her shoulder and down her arm to tangle her fingers in his. 'Last chance to tell me you don't want my hands on you, Sera. Because this is going to complicate things.'

'I want this.' She'd never for one moment not wanted this, from the moment she'd laid eyes on him. 'I crave this,' she whispered, and took the initiative and straddled him, a knee either side of his hips, and slid her hand from his the better to bury both of her hands in his hair. 'I can make it good for you too. So good.'

His shirt had to go. Hers too, and he helped her with that, in between a dozen deep and drugging kisses. Breathing was overrated. His tongue curled around her puckered nipple was not overrated, and then he closed his mouth around it and sucked and she nearly came from that alone. His hands dug into the globes of her behind as he ground up against her, and she gave herself over to sensation and arched into the hardness of his erection and let her head fall back and her hands guide his head towards her other breast.

A soft grunt punched out of her, and he groaned and his hands tightened on her.

Moments later, she was on her back and seeing stars, real ones shining through the glass-domed roof, and Augustus was lifting her legs and removing her shoes and stripping her naked.

She'd been taught what to do, how to please, but she was too caught up in sensation to do any of it.

He started with kisses and gifted them everywhere. The tender curve of her shoulder, the hollow of her armpit and the curve of her breast. Her ribs, the jut of her hip. And then he lifted her leg and started again at her instep and worked his way up. The back of her knee—who knew that would be a go-to zone for squirming? The flesh of her inner thigh. Higher. Black eyes glittering as bold fingers paved the way for his mouth.

She was gone the minute his lips closed over her and his tongue flicked. Whatever this was had been weeks in the making. Every fight, every glance, every moment of pregnant silence between them had been a stroke towards this, and it was wingless flight and fall without a safety net and utterly overwhelming.

It still wasn't enough.

'I need—'

'I know what you need,' he growled. 'And I need a condom.'

'I'm protected.' She opened hazy, glazed grey eyes and caught his face between both hands. 'But there's physical protection to hand if you want to be sure. Be sure.'

She slid out beneath him and crawled naked towards the orgy picture of the pleasure wheel offerings, reaching down to push at something that snapped open, a formerly hidden drawer at the very bottom of that part of the sofa. 'What size?'

What *size*? His brain struggled for clarity until she held up several packets.

'Not that one, not that one, probably this one,' she said, reaching down and plucking a packet from a well-ordered tray. 'You seem rather well formed.'

'You seem rather well stocked.'

He had to laugh. He had to stalk, and push her down on her stomach and start kissing her all over again, even as he reached for the packet in her hand. He hadn't kissed his way down her back yet and that was an oversight he aimed to correct. She was so responsive, so very ready to melt into his touch and give herself over to him. And his need to take was so very big.

He took his time, calling on every bit of the control that had been drilled into him since birth. *Don't lose it. Don't let go. See to the other person's need first because that was service and above all a king served his people. Don't be greedy or entitled.*

Give.

So he gave and gave but she gave it all back and they fed off each other and when he finally breached her, slow and sure, it felt like sliding his soul home.

He stilled, murmuring nonsense against her lips, and she surrendered, eyes never leaving his face as she asked for more.

He took her to the edge, time and time again.

And then he ruthlessly tipped her over the ledge and followed and gave her everything.

CHAPTER EIGHT

'DOES IT HURT?'

Sera couldn't believe how gentle Augustus was being as he bathed her, every stroke of the wash cloth a caress, the water soothing on her skin and the lowlights in the sconces making shadows dance on the walls. He'd been born to care for people, this King, even if he did it from behind self-imposed walls. Get behind the walls of the man and he was overwhelmingly responsive to passion and possession and taking overwhelmingly good care of the woman in his arms.

'It doesn't hurt,' she assured him as he dragged the wash cloth slowly over her centre folds. She'd been a virgin, yes, but her life to date had been an active one and penetration hadn't hurt her the way she'd been warned it might. If the lover was careless or in too much of a hurry.

Augustus had been neither.

'I liked it very much,' she offered and thought to win a smile from him, but he didn't smile.

'Guess you're in the right profession, then.'

Her smile faltered. 'I guess so.'

'Sera—'

But she didn't want to hear what that roughened, sex-soaked voice had to say next. Didn't want to spoil this night with politics or reality or the sure knowledge that she was never going to get to keep this man on a permanent basis. She told herself she didn't want to keep him. That what he'd given her was enough. That she could still walk away from him with her heart intact.

She tried to believe it.

She put her finger to his mouth to silence him, and when he put his hand to her wrist and drew her finger away, she replaced it with her mouth. 'There's more we could do,' she whispered against his lips. He'd been tender with her but she knew there was more. The fingers at her wrist tightened. 'You know there's more you could teach me.'

'Eager.'

'I've been waiting a long time.'

'For me?' This time when he caressed her folds the wash cloth was gone. 'Or for sex?'

'All of it. I didn't expect to want you as much as I do. I could kiss you for hours.' No one had ever told her she'd feel like this. 'Soft and gentle.' Because he had been so very, very gentle with her. Taking care of her pleasure before his own. Reining himself in. 'Or not. Let's try not.'

He claimed her lips with his in a punishing kiss that she returned in full measure. Slick-scraping and filthy, it sent a lightning arc straight through her. And the passion grew.

With a rough fist in his wet hair, she dragged his lips from hers. 'You've seen me dance with swords. You know I'm not going to break.' She knew where she was going with this and it was like stepping off a ledge with a trapeze swing in hand and no knowledge at all of where they might land. 'You know we're not going to be able to have this for ever, but we do have tonight and I want you inside me again, cursing me because you've never had it so good. Ride me till you scream. Or I scream. Take me apart and put me back together again with a piece of you in me.' He was on board with every loaded word, if his glittering, hooded gaze and his iron-hard erection was any indication. 'So do me a favour and this time don't hold back.'

He carried her, wet and wanting, to an alcove filled with pillows and throw rugs and all
manner of oils and unguents.

And this time he didn't hold back.

CHAPTER NINE

AUGUSTUS STRODE INTO his office in a mood that ran blacker than usual. He'd woken alone in Sera's quarters, with a breakfast tray beside him and a blanket draped over his nakedness. They'd finally made it to her bed during the night. Sleep had overtaken him at some point after that. There'd been a note on the pillow next to his head. *Exercising*, was all the note said. A morning ritual for his courtesan of the High Reaches. No matter what.

He'd left a similar note on the pillow requesting her company mid-morning. He had a lunch date he couldn't get out of. With Katerina DeLitt.

He stalked to the coffee corner in the outer office and poured a cup for himself in silence. Lukewarm coffee was his friend.

His secretary cleared his throat and Augustus spared him a glance and there was something off in the older man's gaze—but how could he know?

Granted, the man knew practically everything, but still…

Did he have *I lost my mind and my heart last night* written on his forehead?

'Morning,' he muttered.

'You're late,' the older man said.

Augustus nodded. Instead of taking a quick morning shower, he'd lingered in that damned bathing pool of Sera's, working the kinks out of his body and hoping she'd turn up. She hadn't.

The older man handed him a file and Augustus took it. 'What's this?'

'The investigative report on Lady Sera's mother arrived last night, hand-delivered.'

'Sounds ominous.'

'My investigator judged the information to be of extreme sensitivity so he went old school, helped by the fact that he's seventy years old and *is* old school. The report is hand-written; no digital copies exist and he cleaned up as he went.'

'Meaning?'

'Meaning no one's ever going to find that information again unless they read the file you're holding. You've paid handsomely for the information and that service, by the way. Enough to send an old military-hero-turned-investigator into welcome retirement.'

'I live to serve.' Augustus took the folder from the other man with a frown. He dealt with classified information on a daily basis. He'd never read a hand-written report before. 'Is the information really that sensitive?'

'I doubt it'll start a war. I suspect it'd come as a shock to some of the people involved. Perhaps not all.'

'Be cryptic, then. What do I have on at eleven? Can we clear some space for a meeting with Sera?'

'Another costume tour of the brothels? Circus arts for children? Tortoise races?'

Augustus allowed himself a smile. 'Not yet. And I'm going to need more coffee. Double shot. Hot.'

He went to his office and shut the door behind him, slapped the file down on his desk. His desk was big, black and imposing and his chair was fit for a king and significantly more comfortable. The room was cold, his sister was always complaining of it, but he found it stopped people from lingering overlong and the less they lingered, the more work he got done.

The first half hour of his day was always dedicated to reading. Daily reports sat waiting for him in a tidy pile, arranged in order of importance. He could have read them on his computer just as easily, but there was something about the ritual of paper copies and the pile getting smaller as he worked his way through them that appealed to him. There was an end to that pile of papers, whereas digital news was never-ending. Even if he was deluding himself, he liked to think that his workload had an end-point.

Sera's mother had loved a man, an abusive man, and had a child by him. Sera had already told him this. But she'd never mentioned names, and if he was contemplating marriage to her—which, God help him, he was—he wanted no surprises.

Sera didn't know what to expect when she walked into Augustus's office at exactly eleven a.m. She'd left him sleeping soundly in her quarters because she hadn't known how to deal with him after a night like the one they'd just shared. She still didn't know how to deal with him. But she crossed the cold room and took a seat in the chair placed strategically on the opposite side of his gleaming black desk and tried not to fidget beneath his impenetrable black-eyed gaze.

Gone was his openness of last night and the defencelessness he'd exposed in his sleep. The tousled hair and the boneless weight of his body in her bed. The long, dark lashes fanning delicately over the skin beneath his eyes. He'd been beautiful in his sleep. Softer and more boyish and she'd looked her fill in case she never got to see it again. Some of the things they'd done last night… Skin to skin with heaven in between.

She'd asked for it. She had asked for it. And she had received. 'Morning.'

He quirked a brow and returned her greeting and asked if she wanted some coffee.

She didn't. 'You wanted to see me?'

'For several reasons, not all of them concerning business.' A crack appeared in his regal regard. A flicker of something that might have been concern. 'How are you this morning?'

She felt as if she'd been skewered with a hot buttered sword, had begged for more and been given it. Should she say that? She might have said it to the man. Not to the King.

'So-so,' she said instead. 'Ari chose not to call on me to spar with him this morning. He tells me my concentration's off.'

'Does he know I stayed the night?'

'He's head of my security detail. Of course he knows. Are you worried he'll gossip?'

'No.' Augustus didn't look worried. 'If there's one thing I'm learning about the Order of the Kite, it's how well they can keep secrets. If I wasn't increasingly wary of the lot of you I'd be impressed.'

'If you want to know more about the Order, ask.' She was serious. She'd been handing out historical information ever since she'd got here. 'There's not a lot more left to tell.'

'Really?' The huffing sound he made was an irritated one. 'I had two reports cross my desk this morning, both of them concerning you. One of them informs me that before you came here you were the Chief Financial Officer for a global not-for-profit organisation that distributes over half a billion dollars each year to charities. Lady Lianthe controls the company—which I assume is connected to the Order of the Kite.'

Sera nodded. All of this was public knowledge, or at least accessible knowledge if you knew where to look.

'You were being groomed to replace her,' he said next.

'I was, yes.' She squared her shoulders and

avoided glancing at the report beneath his hand in favour of studying the hand itself. Long fingers, broad base and a signet ring with the royal crest on his middle finger. A kernel of need began to heat deep inside her. Those fingers were magic.

'And here I was trying to turn you into a humble employee so you'd have something more than courtesan to show on your résumé when you left here. More fool me.'

He was angry this morning. Clipped vowels, exact pronunciation. Sera eyed him warily.

'I have no complaints about the work I do here,' she said. 'The charity programme here has been honed over centuries, much like the one the Order oversees, and it's been illuminating to compare and contrast the similarities and differences. They're both good. Different, but good. Besides, you know why I'm here. There is no secret. I didn't come here to court business opportunities. I came here to honour an ancient accord between my people and yours and repay a personal debt I've been accruing since I was seven. I win, Augustus. You keep implying I'm here under duress. You're wrong. I'm here because I choose to be.'

He had the best sexy brooding face she'd

ever seen. 'And where does last night factor into all this winning?'

'Last night can be whatever you want it to be. Forgotten. Repeated. Picked apart until it bleeds.' She was predicting the latter and sought to head him off. 'I enjoyed it.'

'You were a virgin.'

'And?'

'And now you're not.'

Apparently she wasn't the only one with slow brain cells this morning. 'I'll celebrate later. First let me reassure you that I have no regrets, no inclination to tell anyone else what transpired between us and no plans to force you to marry me now that you've claimed my precious virginity.' He looked highly sceptical and Sera bit back a sigh. She had no wish to trap him. That had never been the goal here. Helping him address his needs had been the goal and she was doing that, wasn't she?

Frustration looked remarkably like arousal on him. 'So you *don't* want to marry me?'

Panic hit her hard and fast. 'That's not even on the table. Marriage isn't for the likes of me. Courtesans don't marry.'

'Don't they?' He was getting colder by the second. 'Is it formally not allowed or is it something you personally just don't want to do?'

'You're angry with me.'

'Sharp as ever,' he clipped. 'Answer the question.'

'I've never considered marrying you.' She kept her voice even but it was a near thing. 'Courtesans and kings can be intimate, no question. They often grow quite fond of each other. I'm fond of you.' *Liar—you're in love with him.* 'But a wife's role is very different to that of a courtesan.'

'Really?' She hated his mockery. He did it so well. 'How so? You're already bound to me and under my protection.'

'For a time,' she injected.

'You take on hostess roles, offer me counsel and share my bed.' His lips twisted. 'And you're fond of me.'

She was. Very. 'Augustus, you're a king. I'm nobody. A trained companion.'

'You have connections worldwide and a powerful political faction behind you. You're not nobody.'

She searched for another excuse. 'Your people would never accept me.'

'Wouldn't they? Because, given the press you receive, I'd say you have a better than fair chance they're going to love you.'

'Because I'm an oddity. A throwback curiosity with a sharp brain, a pretty face and interesting clothes.'

'You're making my argument for me.'

She had other arguments. 'You want love. That's why you've stayed single so long. I can't give you that.' Her mother had loved deeply and paid a dreadful price. Sera had paid that price too and had no wish to repeat the experience. 'I won't.'

'What exactly is it you think we did last night, Sera?'

'It was good, I don't deny it. But I've been trained to please.'

Last night...what you did with him? That was love, a little voice told her helpfully. *Are you really going to deny that?*

'My mother loved and look where it got her,' she said doggedly. 'Even when she left him she couldn't escape him. She was never *free*. One day I'm going to be free. If I were to marry you I'd never be free. That other role—'

'*Wife,*' he offered, not at all helpfully. 'Queen Consort. Mother of Kings. Or Queens. Princes and Princesses.' His eyes slayed her with his intensity. 'Heart of a nation.'

Yeah. That. 'I'd never be free.' She retreated into silence. So did he. While the tension in the room threatened to choke her completely.

'Right.' Bitterness tinged his voice. 'Not as if you want to be royal. Which brings me to the second report on my desk. If you wanted to be royal, all you'd have to do is tell people who your father is.'

Sera swallowed hard, her mouth suddenly dry. 'What do you mean?'

He tapped at the folder and her gaze was inevitably drawn to it. 'I mean you're a king's daughter by blood. You simply choose not to acknowledge it.'

He couldn't know that. No one knew that.

'The only time my late mother spoke of my father, she spoke fearfully and never by name,' she offered steadily. 'She said he was a monster who had no time for daughters and I believed her. I don't know who he is but, even if I did, why would I want to acknowledge a man such as that as my father, high-born or not?'

Augustus leaned forward, elbows on the table. 'You know exactly who I'm talking about.'

She'd pieced it together over the years, yes, and then *held her tongue*. Confiding in no one. She wondered if ants felt like this when put beneath a microscope and burned. 'My birth certificate says *father unknown*.'

'Your father died recently. Your half-brother

is a king and as a child you went to school with your half-sister. *If* she's a half-sister. Who sired *her* is a matter of speculation. It could have been the King's brother rather than the King. The point is, you have family. A royal family.'

And she wanted no part of it. 'You have *no proof* of any of this.'

'Haven't I?'

'Augustus, please. Leave it alone. It benefits no one.'

'You know who he is.'

Yes. 'I know nothing.'

'You're lying. You're a royal daughter of Byzenmaach. Does Cas's sister know who you are?'

'Claudia is my *friend.*' Sera stood, incapable of sitting still any longer. 'If my father is who you say he is, then you know he had no use for daughters. The *world* knows this. Yes, my mother was sent to contain him when he began to mistreat his wife. She was to offer other activities for him to focus on, less damaging ways to vent his anger, and she did but he was beyond her control. She failed, and fled and hid and I'm *glad.* I take no pride in the blood running through my veins—and you're only assuming it's his. The man was a tyrant and a murderer. His son, bless us all, is a far better man than he ever was and Byzenmaach is now in good hands. What would I add to that? What could possibly be gained?'

'Power,' he offered.

'I *have* power.'

'Royal status.'

'A noose around my neck.'

'Family,' he said softly, and at this she broke years of deportment training to wrap her arms around her waist and hunch forward as if preventing her stomach from falling out.

'I already have a family,' she whispered, and tried not to think of the pictures in the paper she'd seen recently. Casimir of Byzenmaach, half-brother, wholly in love with his new bride and bastard daughter. A king whose sister had recently returned from exile to claim her rightful place. 'I am Sera Boreas of the High Reaches, daughter of Yuna, pupil of Lianthe, member of the Order of the Kite, and courtesan until you release me. I need no royal titles. I want no royal duties.'

'Not even for me?'

'I don't know what you want from me!' she cried.

'Yes, you do. I've been saying it all along. I don't need a courtesan, Sera, I need a wife. And you, for all that you'll service me while

I'm looking for one, aren't interested in the position. For what it's worth, I don't blame you. You have the world at your feet. Why take on royal duties when you don't have to?' His face hardened. 'But you can't stay here any more. I won't look elsewhere while you're here. And it appears I do need to look elsewhere.'

She stood immobile. 'I can't leave. The accord—'

'You can leave. In fact, I insist.'

He sat so still and silent. She couldn't read him. She didn't know what to say to him. 'By the terms of the accord—'

'I have the right leverage now to do whatever the hell I want. And, believe me, Sera, and with no disrespect to you or your secret Order, I've had enough.'

If anyone had ever asked Augustus of Arun what it felt like to be in love, he couldn't have told them. He'd never been in love before, not once. Not until Sera Boreas walked out of his office and took his beaten, bleeding heart with her.

He put his hands to his face and took a couple of deep breaths. It didn't hurt any less but breathing was a function of living and he still had to do that.

Sera had chosen freedom over duty. Freedom over *him*, and it was a fair call. Last night had been brilliant but he'd been reading too much into it. Passion did that. Wanting something too much did that. So they'd made love. So what? Courtesans did that. Didn't mean she wanted to stay and be his wife.

He reached for the phone.

'Get my lawyers in here. I'm drafting a written offer of marriage to Katerina DeLitt.' Another proposal that was likely to be rejected but it would serve a purpose and he didn't have to present it to Katerina yet. 'I also need you to find out what Sera weighs, double it, and I want that weight in gold removed from the vaults. I want a copy of my offer of marriage to the Baroness DeLitt and the gold delivered to Lianthe of the High Reaches and I want it done today.' He needed to stitch up the gaping hole where his heart had once been and he didn't need an audience. 'And then I want Sera and her guards escorted from my *goddamn home*. Today.'

CHAPTER TEN

SERA STARED UNCOMPREHENDINGLY at the letter Augustus's private secretary had just handed her. It hadn't taken long to read.

'Lady Sera, you are free to leave,' Augustus's secretary said firmly. 'The terms of the accord have been satisfied, or close enough. I've made arrangements for you and your retinue to stay at a hotel in the city.'

Ari stood beside her, arms crossed and his face impassive. 'It's eleven at night.'

'It's a five-star hotel with round-the-clock check-in,' the older man countered. 'Organised and paid for until the end of the month, should you wish to delay your return to the mountains. They're expecting you.'

'How? How has he satisfied the terms of the accord?' asked Sera.

'The King has an offer of marriage on the table and believes the terms of the accord have been satisfied in principle, milady. Lady Lianthe agrees. *Double* your weight in gold has already been delivered to her.'

'I—' She needed to call Lianthe. She needed to speak to Augustus. 'Is His Majesty in? May I speak with him?' Not that she had any idea what she was going to say. *Thank you? How did you do it? Are you really going to cut me loose, just like that?*

'He's not in.'

There'd been no evening event written into his schedule this morning. Sera knew this because the man standing in front of her had been emailing her Augustus's daily schedule every morning for several weeks.

'May I see him in the morning?'

'His Majesty has a full schedule tomorrow. He needs to finish everything he put on hold today in order to accommodate your wishes.'

'My wishes?'

'Your wish to leave.'

'Right,' she said faintly. 'That wish. The owls—'

'Will be taken care of. Your belongings packed and returned to the High Reaches. There's a palace vehicle at your disposal. It's waiting for you at the south wall entrance.'

Funny how freedom felt a lot like dismissal. Sera nodded. Manners before breakdown.

Discretion over protest. 'I'll leave a letter for His Majesty on my desk. Will you see that he gets it?'

'He'll get it.' The older man seemed to soften and sag. 'The question you should be asking is: will he read it?'

Ari waited until the King's secretary had left the room before turning silently towards her, eyebrow raised.

'I need to ring Lianthe,' she told him. 'Alert the others that we might be on our way.'

He nodded and reached for his phone, heading over towards the entrance doors but staying inside the room where once he might have stood outside the doors to give her more privacy. Sera walked in the opposite direction and made her call from the bedroom.

Lianthe picked up on the second ring.

'Is it true? Have the terms of the accord been satisfied?' Sera asked without preamble.

'Well, he doesn't have a wife and he doesn't have an heir but he does have a valid wedding proposal in play and I have no reason to believe it will be rejected. He also informs me that your presence is no longer required and has threatened to expose your connection to the Byzenmaach throne if I don't agree with him.'

Lianthe drew a heavy breath. 'So I agreed with him. I'm not sure where he got his information from. I can't imagine you told him.'

'I didn't.' Sera closed her eyes and tilted her head towards the sky, only the sky wasn't there; it was only the ceiling. 'He had us investigated.'

'That information's not available.'

'Nonetheless, he got it from somewhere.' The sudden sting of hot tears welled beneath her eyelids. 'He asked me to marry him. And I didn't know what to say.'

'I suspect that says it all.' The other woman's voice was soft and soothing. 'What a pity. I find his utter ruthlessness on your behalf quite admirable. He must be very much in love with you.'

'He's trapped, that's all. He's being forced to take a wife and his heart's not engaged with any of the available candidates. I've watched him. He can drum up polite friendliness towards them if pressed.'

'And what does he drum up for you?'

Stories from his childhood and an insatiable sexual hunger that had left her wrung out and panting. Challenge and temper and unexpected moments of understanding. 'More. But Lianthe, I'm not cut out for love. Courtesans don't love. They serve, willingly, and I have. We were doing well. No one ever said anything about *love*.'

'You have something against it?'

Yes. 'I don't believe it brings happiness.'

'Your mother was an extreme case. She had a soft heart and the man she fell for, he wasn't soft at all.'

'Neither's this one. He's difficult and demanding.' And passionate and protective and a demon in bed. 'And petty and powerful and…' Gorgeous and supportive of her charity schemes and… 'He's a king in need of a queen. There'd be oaths to Crown and country. I'd be accountable for every minute of every day. Who would want that?'

'Who indeed?'

'It's a lifetime sentence of duty and reckoning and being judged. And usually being judged wanting.'

'Indeed.'

'Who'd want that?' she repeated.

'Not you, clearly. You probably wouldn't rise to the occasion at all, even if you loved him. Which you don't.'

'I don't.'

'Well, then.' Lianthe sounded disturbingly cheerful. 'When are you coming home?'

* * *

'Want to talk about it?'

Augustus scowled at his sister and wondered, not for the first time, why he'd allowed her to invite herself to dinner. She said she'd missed him—which he very much doubted, given how busy she was. She'd wanted a catch-up—which usually meant pumping him for information or delicately *revealing* information that might be of interest to him. The fact that he'd banished the only other woman who'd ever come close to providing him with this type of relaxed political conversation was not lost on him. 'Talk about what?'

'The rumour that you've proposed, or are about to propose, to Katerina DeLitt. The abrupt midnight departure of your courtesan.' Moriana waved an airy hand towards him from across the dining room table. 'You choose.'

Sera had left four nights ago. The people of the High Reaches would be coming to collect everything that belonged to them, Lianthe had said, but she hadn't mentioned when. Stepping into the round room only to find Sera not there was driving him insane. The soft hoot of owls mocked him. The tapestry wheel of pleasure haunted him. So many things they hadn't done yet. Perhaps he should be thankful.

'I choose silence.'

Moriana allowed him that silence for all of thirty seconds, and that was only because she had a mouthful of food.

'You want to talk to Theo about it?' she asked when her mouth was empty again. 'Or Benedict? Benedict's surprisingly insightful when it comes to matters of the heart.'

It stood to reason he would be, what with all that practice. 'Thank God he's not here,' Augustus offered drily. 'Sera Boreas has gone, the accord has been honoured to everyone's satisfaction, and I'll be married by the end of the year.'

'So you say. But to whom? And please don't tell me you're madly in love with Katerina. I know you. And you're not.'

'Since when has love ever been a prerequisite for marriage?'

'Since when has love ever *not* been a prerequisite for you?'

'Not everyone is cut out for the kind of love you and Theo share.'

'You're not so different from me.' Moriana raised her chin and regarded him haughtily. 'You want that kind of love—you always have.'

He offered up a careless shrug and cut into

his meal, ignoring his sister's scowl. She hated it when he refused to engage. Said it was a stalling tactic that had no place in open conversation.

'Augustus, I love you. You know this.'

Uh-oh.

'But I've had a dozen calls this week from people here in your palace, begging me to come and strangle you. At which point I would become their ever so reasonable Queen.'

Augustus snorted.

'I'd probably have to renounce Theo to do it, of course, and this baby currently in my belly would probably be kidnapped back and forward between palaces until he ran away and joined the circus, but at least your palace employees wouldn't be suffering.'

'You're pregnant?' She didn't look pregnant, even if she did look more vibrant than usual. He'd put that down to their argument, or the wine she…wasn't drinking. So much for his keen powers of observation. Sera would have caught that one within five minutes of being in the room.

Moriana nodded and offered up a tiny but self-satisfied smile. 'I'm barely nine weeks in. We're keeping it quiet until I'm a little further along, but I wanted to tell you now and in person.'

'Congratulations.' He meant it. 'Are you well?' Was she happy about it?

Theo would be ecstatic with an heir on the way.

'I'm as well as can be, given that I can barely keep dry toast in my stomach before lunchtime. Augustus, I'm so happy. A mother. Me!'

Envy had no place in his heart. His sister was happy and deserved to be. He could wait, and one day it would be his turn to puff with pride and joy because his wife was pregnant. But there was only one woman's face he could see in that particular daydream. Sera, with her slender frame, luminous grey eyes and flawless skin.

The same woman that had chosen freedom over a life spent with him.

He didn't blame her.

He'd done everything in his power to set her free.

'You could go after her now that the accord has been satisfied,' said Moriana, and he blinked because he thought they weren't having this conversation, only apparently they were. 'You always did have trouble with the *she was duty bound to serve you* part.'

'If we're using the argument that Sera's now a free woman, she could come back at any time. Do you see her here?' He didn't need Moriana's answer. 'Neither do I.'

'She hasn't returned to the High Reaches,' Moriana said tentatively.

'Perhaps she's sick of serving them too.'

'I have it on good authority that she's in Byzenmaach, at Cas's Winter fortress.'

'She's *where*?'

'Visiting Cas's sister.' Moriana eyed him with blatant curiosity. 'They know each other. Studied together in the mountains as kids.'

He hadn't told Moriana about Sera's parentage. He hadn't told anyone. He'd tried telling himself that such effective leverage could be used over and over again if he kept it to himself but the truth was he'd never go against Sera's wishes to keep her father's identity a secret and he'd never use that particular leverage again. He was done with it. He was done with *her*.

'So what are you going to name this baby? Have you given it any thought?'

'I've given it no thought at all yet.' Her eyes glinted with sharp humour.

'And the due date is when?'

'Thirty-one weeks from now, apparently.

You could drop in on Claudia or go see Tomas about how to get rid of the remaining owls in the round room. They shouldn't be too hard to catch, seeing as I have it on good authority that you're feeding them.'

'Lies.' All lies. 'And the baby's health? How's the baby's health?' Why couldn't she be one of those expectant mothers that talked of nothing else?

'Good try, brother.' Moriana outright smirked. 'Should you be fortunate enough to be invited to see beyond the veil of Theo's outright terror at the thought of becoming a father, I should warn you he will talk of nothing else but baby names, giving birth and raising children. Honestly, I think it broke his brain.'

It was Augustus's turn to grin outright. 'Really? Theo's gone gaga? I'd like to see that.'

'You have no idea.'

'I'm thrilled for you both.'

Moriana looked positively tearful as she set her cutlery down and reached for her napkin to dab at her eyes. Their late lamented mother would have scolded her twice over. First for her unseemly display of emotion, and then for inappropriate use of tableware. Such scolding would have once sent his sister spinning into the depths of despair but the new, improved Moriana didn't seem to care.

'Have you really proposed to Katerina DeLitt?' she asked, because she was a sneaky, *sneaky* woman, not above using tears to disarm him.

'I've drawn up an offer, yes.'

'Have you sent it?'

It was still sitting on his desk. 'Do you have anything against her?'

'Nothing at all, apart from the fact that you're in love with someone else. As a woman who's been in Katerina DeLitt's position before, she has my utmost sympathy. If you had any sense, you wouldn't even consider proposing to her in your current condition. If she had any sense she'd refuse you.'

'Maybe she will.'

Sera had refused him.

His sister regarded him solemnly. 'Will you at least meet with Sera again before you take such an irrevocable step with someone else?'

He gathered up the icy reserve he rarely wore around his sister and pinned her with his gaze. As dear as she was to him, and pregnant along with it, her interference was unwelcome.

'I didn't want to talk about any of this with you, but I heard you out and now it's your turn to hear me. No, I will not seek out Sera again. I've had my say already and her ambitions do not include becoming my Queen. I will not discuss this with you or anyone else ever again. And if you don't like my answer, feel free to leave.'

CHAPTER ELEVEN

CASIMIR OF BYZENMAACH'S Winter fortress perched atop a mountain pass. Sera had reached out to Claudia and asked if she knew of a place where she could exercise and clear her head and it was a measure of their friendship that the other woman had instantly invited her to stay.

Accepting that invitation without disclosing the secret of her parentage made Sera the worst friend in the world, but up here in the mountain pass, with Tomas's falcons soaring overhead and dawn breaking softly over the horizon, she felt a peace steal over her that she hadn't felt in days.

She finished her forms and bowed to the valley below and the rising sun and turned to find her hostess sitting silently on a rock behind her, watching. So she bowed to her too and watched the other woman smile.

'That was beautiful,' said Claudia. 'But then, you always have been very beautiful.'

'My lot to bear.' Always making waves, being coveted or even despised for no other reason than she'd drawn someone's eye. Glazed stares, suspicious glares and people wanting to possess her.

Augustus had wanted to possess her from the beginning.

It was a miracle, really, that he'd withstood that urge for as long as he had.

'Whose heart have you broken this time?' Claudia asked.

'One does not kiss and tell,' she replied quietly and picked up the towel she'd brought with her and put it to her face.

King Casimir and his family were at their Summer palace in the city, not here. She'd wanted to meet him. She hadn't wanted to meet him. Those two thoughts did not coexist peacefully.

She didn't know what she wanted any more.

Lowering the towel, she closed her eyes and drew fresh breath, feeling at home here, in a way that had everything to do with cool mountain air and not having to view the sky from beneath a web of steel and glass.

No endless dinners, galas and fund-raisers to oversee.

No severely tailored work clothes.

No king to serve.

No duty.

'I don't know what to do any more,' she confessed. 'I have no plans, no direction, no thoughts for the future. I'm finally free and all I'm doing is looking over my shoulder at what I left behind.'

Claudia nodded. 'I know that feeling. Here.' She opened a small basket at her feet. 'I brought breakfast. The food here is amazing.'

Sera spread her towel on the ground and sat cross-legged, and for a time they feasted on meat pastries and sweet milky tea. But Sera wasn't quite ready to let go of her friend's earlier comment. 'Do you ever think you should have stayed in the mountains?'

'I'm of more use to the people of the High Reaches if I'm advocating for them here, so no. I shouldn't have stayed in the mountains.'

'But do you like it here?' Sera watched as the other woman's gaze tracked a falcon in full flight. 'Do they treat you well?'

'They treat me like a princess, because that's what I am. Some treat me like a newfound friend and confidante and I like that. Some can barely look at me but dream of the day I was taken from them, nonetheless. It's not always easy but I'm making my home here.' Claudia reached for a paper napkin. 'I wanted you to meet my niece. Face of an angel and an absolute terror. Wants to be a Samurai this week. I thought you two could bond.'

'I'd like to meet her.' A niece. She blinked back sudden tears.

'Hey.' A warm palm snaked out to cover her forearm. 'What is it?'

'Nothing, I—nothing. I'd like to meet her some day.'

'Hardly a thought to induce tears—although some of the guards here may beg to differ.'

Sera smiled, as she was meant to smile. 'Thank you for inviting me here.'

'Stay as long as you dare.'

'Another day, perhaps. After that I don't know. I need to keep moving.' Searching, so that she didn't keep remembering nights full of politicking and quiet confidences and one night in particular when she and Augustus had forgotten their roles and let honesty rule them.

'May I do a visualisation exercise with you?' Claudia reached out and took both of Sera's hands in hers. 'It's one I've found useful whenever I find myself adrift. Close your eyes.'

Sera nodded and closed her eyes.

'You're standing at a crossroads. Seven paths to choose from, radiating out in all directions. Some safe, because you know where they lead. Some bright and beckoning and full of new adventures. Others dark and seductively forbidding. On some paths you can see family in the distance and maybe you're not sure of your welcome because they look so happy. What else could they possibly need?'

Sera opened her eyes and searched the other woman's face for some sign that she *knew*.

And found nothing.

'Close your eyes.' Claudia moved her thumbs in soothing circles over Sera's skin. 'Someone stands beside you at that crossroads. Someone you'll never leave behind because you carry them in your heart like a talisman. Someone whose path was chosen for them the minute they were born. They couldn't follow you even if they wanted to. All they can do is be there at the crossroads where your lives intersect and watch you make your choice and let you go. They'll fight for your right to do that, you see. Of all the gifts they can give you, it's the most expensive.'

Sera trembled. 'I know who you're talking about.'

'Do you? Because it could be anyone. It could be me.'

Sera snapped her eyes open and saw nothing but love and gentle understanding.

'It could be me saying I'm right here and ready to be whatever you need me to be,' Claudia repeated quietly. 'Close your eyes and breathe.'

Sera closed her eyes and breathed.

'Whenever I do this exercise I see Tomas beside me. Whoever heard of a princess and a falconer? He won't even lay a hand on me, can hardly bear to look at me, but I swear to you I'm laying down a new path for us, brick by brick, just in case he ever wants to walk my way. It's not so easy to live a royal life, you see, and those already there will never force the issue. You don't need to mention my regard for Tomas to him, by the way, unless it comes up in conversation. At which point, go for it and use embellishments.'

Sera opened one eye and arched her brow.

'Shut it. No winking,' her sister of the heart replied with a tiny grin. 'I'm trying so hard not to make this about me. Close your eyes and open your heart.'

Sera obeyed.

'I know there's someone there beside you at

your crossroads. I know you can't move forward without resolving your feelings for them. Doing that is your next step and it might be the most important step you ever take.' Claudia moved forward; Sera could feel it even if she couldn't see it. The other woman's cheek brushed hers, comfort, solidarity and warmth, as she whispered, 'You know who you see.'

They walked back down the mountain in the crisp morning air, Claudia looking skyward more than once and smiling softly when a falcon appeared and circled above. 'They questioned Tomas for days after I disappeared,' Claudia told Sera. 'He was eight years old and the last person to see me and they grilled him over and over again, with no mercy given for the fact that he too was a child.'

'And now he uses falcons to track your every movement?'

'Not my every movement.' Claudia sprang from one step to the next, her feet sure as they made their way down the rocky path. 'He's been training himself to wait longer and longer each time I come up here before flying one of his hunting hawks to find out where I am. We're up to almost an hour.'

'And do you help him with the birds?'

'You know I do.' Claudia had skills of her own in that area. 'Watching that man work is a pleasure I have no words for.'

'And how will you manage to steer him towards romance if you're the Princess in the castle and he's but a mere falconer?'

'By putting my own spin on this Princess gig and getting out of the castle a lot,' Claudia offered drily. 'It helps that Cas is so utterly overcome by my return that he lets me do whatever I want.'

'He didn't reprimand you for staying away?'

Claudia might have been kidnapped as a child—for her own good, as it turned out—but she'd had chances to return over the years and had never done so. Not until her father had died and her brother had taken the throne.

'It wasn't safe for me here. You know that.'

'But it is now.'

Claudia nodded and looked to the sky and let the early morning light caress her face. 'It is now.'

Coffee was served on their return, set up on a little table on a balcony overlooking a walled garden. There was also fresh fruit and bread, and an array of northern delicacies to tempt them.

'Is this all for us?' asked Sera because,

frankly, half a dozen more people could have joined them and it still would have been too much food for one sitting.

'They're making up for all the years I was gone. It's what people do around here.'

'Every day?'

'Every damn day.' Claudia reached for a royal blue folder sitting on the table. 'Mind if I look through my morning mail? The palace keeps me informed as to the news of the day.'

'And you trust this information?'

Claudia laughed. 'Oh, Sera. The look on your face. If something of interest comes up I look into it. Did you not rely on the Arunian palace for information?'

'Not really. I have my own sources.'

'I find these ones useful and I don't have to go looking for them. They even present them in order of palace importance. Very informative in itself, would you not say? Take this one, for example: it's item one and it's a note from the desk of Moriana of Liesendaach, formerly of Arun, telling Cas that there's been an assassination attempt on her brother but rumour of his death is a gross exaggeration. Is that not good to know?'

'What?'

Claudia passed the sheet of paper over without further comment, and picked up the next item. 'And here's what the tabloids have to say. Hmm. Your good King was in a bad part of the city last night. Two people in custody, Augustus and a minor in intensive care.'

'A minor?' Sera wasn't tracking too well any more. Hadn't been since the words *Augustus* and *death* had been mentioned in the same breath.

'Here.' Claudia passed that one to Sera too before picking up her coffee in one hand and sifting quickly through the others. 'That's all the information I have. Do you have anyone you can get more information from?'

'Not at this hour.' It was still too early for regular workday hours, and for all that Augustus's executive secretary often stayed late, he rarely began his day before nine. 'Unless the entire communications team has been called in to deal with this. Then there might be someone there willing to give me more information.'

'Would you like to use one of our phones?' Sera asked.

'They'll think the call is coming from the Byzenmaach King.'

Claudia raised a dark brow. 'And? Not as if there aren't advantages to that approach.'

The woman had a point.

She found a phone and made the call to Augustus's office number and waited impatiently for someone to pick up.

The call appeared to get diverted and Augustus's secretary answered on the sixth ring, his voice curtly polite and the strain in it evident.

'It's Sera,' she said.

Silence.

'I'm staying at the Winter fortress in Byzenmaach and heard the news this morning.'

More silence.

Don't hang up... 'How is he?' She cleared her throat. 'Please.'

Claudia was watching her from the doorway. Ari stood sentry on the other side of the room, silently watching them both.

'He's in intensive care,' the older man said finally and Sera let her head droop so her hair curtained her face.

'And his condition?'

'He needs someone to fight for him.'

'I can fight,' she said, blinking back tears. 'I know how to fight.'

'Yes, I know. We all know that. But, if I may be so bold, don't come back if you're not planning to stay. He let you go once because that's what you said you wanted and it nearly destroyed him. Don't make him go through that again.'

'I won't.'

'Would you like to put that in writing?'

'If you tell me where he is, I'll put it on a billboard.'

'He's at the Sisters of Mercy Hospital in the capital. They have a helipad, and I assume you have access to a helicopter and a pilot. Tell them to go through me and I'll clear your way for landing.'

It was more welcome than she'd ever hoped for. 'You're probably going to get into trouble for this.'

'I probably am,' he countered drily.

'That's a debt you'll be able to collect on, should you ever need something from me in the future.'

'Do you still have your guards with you?'

'Yes.'

'Then I'm calling that debt in right now. Bring them. The King's head of security quit this morning in a fit of temper. There's an opening.'

'I'll bring them.' She couldn't resist the next question. 'What happened?'

'Which version would you like, milady?'

'Your version.' She trusted the older man's take on palace events.

'In that case, the answer's very simple. Most

people have a healthy sense of self-preservation. My King has lost his.'

It took three tries to put the phone back in its cradle and the third time Claudia's hand was guiding her. 'I need a helicopter,' she said.

'Then you shall have one.'

'And a pilot.'

'I shall fly you myself.'

Which was how Sera managed to get from Byzenmaach's Winter fortress to the Sisters of Mercy Hospital in just over an hour, her guards flanking her as she strode from the helipad towards the building. She had her travelling cloak on but didn't bother with the hood. Memorable entries were her speciality, and she had every intention of brazening this one out.

Augustus's secretary stood waiting for her and opened the door as she approached.

'How is he?' A question that carried with it everything her world had narrowed down to. Because there was only one person she wanted to walk beside in this world and if he wasn't alive...

If she never got that chance...

All the colours of the world would be gone.

'Please. How is he?'

'Follow me,' he said. He avoided her gaze and supplied no other answer. Maybe he had no

answer for her. 'Is his sister here? His father?'
Had Augustus's next of kin been gathered?

'They're about.' The older man swept them
through a long hallway with security guards at
either end. Guards who nodded and straightened to attention as they passed by. She thought
Ari's barely leashed displeasure at their care-
lessness in letting an assassin get close enough
to their King to do damage might have something to do with it. That or her own scathing,
stormy gaze.

'Ari and Tun will relieve the guard detail on
the door to the critical care unit,' she said, and
smiled tightly when the old courtier blinked at
her sheer hide. 'You were the one who wanted
them here. No one said anything about you
commanding them.'

'Perhaps you will allow His Majesty's
guards to brief your men on what actually happened last night before you sweep them aside,'
the older man advised. 'The King occasionally
goes into the city by himself and in disguise.
He did this last night.'

'And you *let* him?'

'Freedom's irresistible to those who've never
had it.' They'd reached the end of yet another
long corridor with guards stationed at either
end. 'You can go in.'

'Is anyone in there with him?' It wasn't that she was putting off walking through those doors. She simply wanted to be prepared for whoever she might find.

'His sister's just stepped out.'

There was never going to be a better time.

There was one bed in the room she entered and it was empty, machines switched off and the bottom sheet rumpled, the top sheet pushed aside. Augustus stood to one side of the window on the opposite side of the room, his face pale and wan, his chest bare, his shoulder bandaged and his left arm strapped tightly to his chest.

His eyes widened at the sight of her.

'Hello,' she said awkwardly, caught completely off guard. Not that the sight of him standing there didn't fill her heart to overflowing, but this really wasn't the kind of intensive care she'd imagined. 'I… Ah, you can stand.'

He raised a quizzical eyebrow.

'And…uh…walk. That's good. Brilliant recovery.' She'd been had, but right now she didn't give a damn. 'So good.'

'What are you doing here?' If she was drinking him in with her eyes, he was doing much the same to her.

'I was—'

In the area and just thought she'd drop by? Hardly.

'That is to say—'

He was waiting for her to say.

'I was visiting Claudia, my friend who is not my sister, and she has this mountain…'

He looked sceptical. 'Of course it's not her mountain, but it's a mountain nonetheless, and I was up there thinking about you, and me, and whether there could ever be a "you *and* me" that wasn't all about honour and duty and sacrifice. A you and me that *does* involve those things, sure,' she said, and contradicted herself completely and stumbled on regardless. 'Because you're you and there's no getting away from your duty as King, but above all that, or maybe underneath it, I was wondering if there might be a "*you and me*" who could be together and we could make a point of building some freedom into our lives, keeping the courtesan's quarters open as a place where you can be you and I can be me, and there could be holidays in the mountains and I could show you things you've never seen. And maybe at some point, if you haven't already proposed to Katerina DeLitt, that is, we could talk about you marrying me.' She tailed off, wishing he'd say something. 'Because of love.'

'Was that supposed to make sense?'

Yes, yes, it was, and if it hadn't she'd try again. 'I'm in love with you.'

'Why?' The tiniest tilt of his lips gave her the courage she needed to keep going.

'Because you let me in, even though you knew this was going to get messy. Because you let me try and be all those dozen different things I was taught to be, no matter the cost to yourself. Because you put my needs before yours and fought for my right to be free in a way you can never be. And I *am* free now and I'm still being selfish, because when I heard you'd been hurt there was only one place I wanted to be. So here I am.'

And there he stood.

'Of course, you might not have much use any more for the love of a former courtesan and that's okay too.'

'No reciprocation required?' he asked softly.

'No. That's not love. Love is standing here and feeling so much relief and joy that you *are* okay. And then turning around and walking out that door if you ask me to.'

She wanted to stay. She so badly wanted to touch him. But she didn't have the right to.

'Come here,' he said and she walked closer and fought every twitchy bit of muscle memory not to sink to the floor at his feet. He'd never wanted that from her.

'If there's such a thing as love at first sight, I felt it the first time I ever saw you.' He touched his fingers to the tie at her neck and tugged it loose and then used both hands to push her travelling cloak from her shoulders until it pooled in a puddle at her feet. 'First time you ever curtseyed for me, I was torn between wanting to keep you there for ever and never wanting you to lower yourself in front of me again because I wanted an equal. I *needed* an equal. And you stayed and triumphed, no matter what I threw at you, and I realised I'd finally found one.' He traced the line of her cheek with the backs of his fingers. 'Always knew I'd have to let you go.'

'You did.'

'And yet here you are.' He threaded his fingers through her hair. 'And I think you should know that I have no intention of ever letting you go again.' He kissed her gently at first and then somehow it became all-consuming.

They were both breathing raggedly when finally he broke the kiss. He rested his forehead against hers and huffed a laugh before taking a determined step back. 'I had a plan for if you ever came back. It involved rather more clothes and no bullet wounds on my part, and there was possibly a fantasy moment of you wearing ancient slave jewellery mixed up in there somehow, but I did have a plan and it went something like this. I love you. I want you by my side from this day forward and not as my courtesan or employee.'

He got down on bended knee and tugged his ring from his finger and held it out to her. It was a dark blue cabochon sapphire with the royal insignia of Arun overlaid in diamonds. 'This one's heavy, I know, but it's yours if you'll take it. There'll be other rings, I promise. Sera, will you marry me?'

'Yes.' A lifetime of royal duty in exchange for the opportunity to walk beside the man she loved and who loved her in return. 'Yes, I will.'

He put the ring on her finger and she looked at it and then at him. 'I know what you mean now about having someone kneel at your feet. It's very disconcerting having all sorts of thoughts running through your mind about what they might do while they're there.'

'Tell me about it,' he said with a glint in his eye that promised exploration. 'And don't spare the details.'

'Another time, perhaps. Once you've fully recovered from your...did you say *bullet wounds*?'

'I may have been an idiot in your absence. You're likely to hear about it at some point. I believe there's a *Bring Sera Back* petition circulating through the palace as we speak. Or perhaps everybody's signed it by now. There was a jar circulating too. People were putting gold jewellery into it, trying to raise your bodyweight in gold as an incentive to woo you back.'

Sera blinked. 'They what?'

'Good thing there's not much of you.'

A knock on the door preceded the entry of Moriana of Liesendaach, formerly of Arun. She took one look at Sera and her brother, still on bended knee, and said, 'Oh, now that's a pretty look.'

'Do you *mind*?' Augustus asked her.

'Oh, no. Not at all. Please. Continue. Don't mind me.' Moriana waved away his concerns. 'Hi, Sera.'

Sera waved and the ring on her finger glinted.

Moriana's smile broadened. 'Does this mean I can have my six gold bracelets and Theo's two golden goblets back? Because Theo did, in fact, get into trouble for donating those goblets to the cause. Not only are they insanely heavy, apparently they're two thousand years old.'

Sera leaned forward and put her lips to Augustus's ear. 'I think you should get up now,' she whispered. 'I promise to make it worth your while later.'

The smile of unfiltered joy he bestowed on her was one she wanted to see at least once every day for the rest of her life.

'We're getting married,' Augustus said.

Moriana rolled her eyes but her smile almost rivalled her brother's. 'I never would have guessed.'

'And I need to speak with my future wife about exactly how quickly we can make that happen,' he continued regally and pointed towards the door.

'I can help you there.' Moriana was enjoying herself way too much. 'Royal weddings take time. Months. Years! And involve processions.'

'Out!' He sounded so commanding.

'In the mountains of the High Reaches there's a ceremony called a binding,' Sera offered quietly. 'It involves two people pledging their hearts into the other's safe keeping. There are four witnesses, one for each point of the compass. It's very simple. Will you do it with me?'

'I'll do it today and every day for the rest of my life,' he promised, and touched his lips to hers.

When Sera finally surfaced, Moriana was gone and the door to the room was firmly closed.

'How soon can we break you out of here?' she asked, and placed a gentle hand to his shoulder and then to his heart.

'They're being overly cautious,' he grumbled. 'I can be out of here tonight.'

Uh-huh. She'd like to see him try.

'One week,' she promised. 'One week today and with the mountains as our witness I will bind my heart to you.'

EPILOGUE

AUGUSTUS STOOD DRAPED in the ceremonial black furs that also served to keep the bitter cold at bay. He wore his royal uniform beneath the borrowed cloak because, for all that he was standing on a mountain with a blizzard closing in, he was still the King of Arun and carried the hopes of his people with him.

He'd been in the mountains for two days and had stayed in a sprawling fortress every bit as grand as any he'd ever stayed in. Sera had shown him the horses, the falcons, the temples and the steps carved into a mountain path that wove its way ever skyward in suicidal fashion. Only for her had he risen and bathed and dressed before dawn and climbed those icy steps, grateful for the burning torches carried by others and the chain ropes beaten into the rock centuries ago and the heavy-duty gloves lent to him by Ari this morning.

A High Reaches binding was not for those who lacked courage and the journey there was part of the process.

His sister and her unborn babe were here, swathed in ceremonial garb and red-gold furs. She would take the East point on the compass, the new dawn. The Lady Lianthe stood to the North, a guiding light, the voice of experience. His father stood to the South, the foundation stone for all that would grow. Princess Claudia of Byzenmaach took the West point and, while darkness and betrayal rode with her as part of her past, she wore love like a shield and had cloaked herself in purest white.

The sky overhead was a vivid blue, a perfect complement to the snowy white and the occasional slash of rocky grey.

There were the four points of the compass, an invisible circle connecting them, and only two sets of footprints within that circle.

They met at the centre, where a goblet of melted snow sat on a stony plinth, and if Theo thought his goblets were heavy they had nothing on this one.

Sera wore a cloak of grey to match her eyes and he couldn't wait to see what was under it. Something similar to bridal wear, she'd told him demurely. Beyond that, he'd have to wait and see.

Her hair had been coiled atop her head and dressed with diamonds.

She wore a fine platinum necklace, matching earrings and the royal ring he'd given her one week earlier in lieu of an engagement ring.

She was loving and giving and his and he'd never felt more blessed.

There would be a wedding, of course. A royal one with cavalries and balconies and a kiss in full view of the people. It was expected. It was tradition. But this…this moment here was deeply, emphatically personal. Simple words meant for no one but the one receiving them.

Four witnesses, a sacred mountain, a cup full of water and a vivid blue sky.

And then Sera spoke.

'My heart is pure and true and yours,' she told him. 'I offer it from a position of knowledge, power and freedom.'

It was all he'd ever hoped for.

'I accept this priceless gift and I will never let you down,' he promised and drank from the goblet.

And then it was his turn to say the words. 'My heart is steadfast and often guarded because it carries with it the weight of a nation but to you I offer it freely and without reservation. It's yours.'

'I accept this priceless gift,' she said, and drained her goblet. 'And, let all here bear witness, I will never let you down.'

* * * * *

If you enjoyed
Untouched Queen by Royal Command
you're sure to enjoy the first two instalments in Kelly Hunter's
Claimed by a King quartet!

Shock Heir for the Crown Prince
Convenient Bride for the King

Available now!